VELLAAYI

Written by

K V RAJA SARAVANAN

Translated by

NAVEEN ITHIKKAT

Paintings by

MARY JANE

Cover Design and 'World of Vellaayi' Illustration by

SUMANT DUBEY

Dancer in Cover Photo

DR. JANAKI RANGARAJAN

Photo of Namperumal

R.K LAKSHMI

INTERNATIONAL EDITION

ISBN 9798588061995

To the people of Srirangam, who consider the Lord as a member of their own family.

Disclaimer

This novel is a work of fiction. Although it is based on true incidents, we have taken creative liberties to fictionalize the missing pages of history. It is not our intention to hurt anyone's sentiments through this endeavour.

Contents

Foreword by

Dr. Janaki Rangarajan

It is my pleasure and honour to write the foreword for this wonderful book written so lucidly by Thiru. Raja Saravanan and translated by Thiru. Naveen Ithikkat.

As I read the book, one thing was very evident, the author's innate love for Andal and Srirangam. The simple unhurried beauty and love that surrounds Vellaayi's life are reflected very organically in the author's writing. But what makes the story line very interesting and gripping is the nuanced understanding and description of the historical facts, people, rituals, social practices, culture and nature itself. The way the author has described all of them, down to the minutest details, is very captivating, accurate, and gives a lot of depth to the story of Vellaayi. The surrender and sacrifice of Vellaayi is a must-read and something that is important to understand and reflect upon.

I truly enjoyed reading "Vellaayi" and wish Thiru. Raja Saravanan and Thiru. Naveen Ithikkat all the best for their future endeavors.

Dr. Janaki Rangarajan

Bharatanatyam exponent

Date: 11-Nov-20

Preface

Standing atop the roof of the Srirangam temple complex and looking at the perfectly aligned gopurams on the four sides of the temple, I feel as if someone has brought Vishnu's abode in heaven down here to earth. Curious to learn more about this beautiful temple, I turn the pages of Srirangam's history - and find surprises on every page! The feeling of having chanced upon an unexpected treasure grows within me, and I start collecting anecdotes of events that have happened here. There seem to be infinite stories about this place - each worth telling. However, this novel is about the story that I felt most motivated to tell.

Although I have come close to writing a Tamil novel before, this is my first one. Novels written by Sujatha have always inspired me. More recently, I had a chance to listen to the works of Amarar Kalki's works in Tamil. The audiobook version of Kalki's novels produced and created by Shri Bombay Kannan and Shri C K Venkatraman have been inspiring as well. Kalki had the ability to take his readers to different time periods in his own unique way. His style of writing has had a lasting effect on me. As a result, I started to write Vellaayi's story.

After writing a few chapters, I had shared it with some of my friends and family. Fortunately, they liked it and encouraged me to write more. Some of my friends joined me at the very beginning, and we worked as a team to create this. Although my friends were distributed across geographies and timezones, technology helped us to collaborate. My friends Lakshmi from Hyderabad (India), and Rukmani from Seattle (USA) helped with the proofreading and improvisation of the Tamil novel. Mary Jane from Chennai (India) created beautiful paintings for each of the chapters that brought the world of Vellaayi to life. We then created an audio sample of the novel and shared it with some friends. As we got positive responses, it encouraged us to complete the novel in audio format. Priya from San Jose (USA) narrated the story of Vellaayi in audio format. Rukmani from Seattle (USA), and Srinivas Sampath from Bangalore (India) sang the pasurams in the chapters. Ashok Natarajan from Bangalore (India) mixed and mastered the final audio tracks for publishing. Ponraj from Chennai (India) did the proofreading for the draft version of the Tamil novel.

On the request of many of my non-Tamil speaking friends, I decided to create the English version of this novel. My childhood friend Naveen Ithikkat is someone whom I have always looked up to since my school days for his proficiency in English. I sincerely hoped he would agree to do this translation. When I spoke to him about my desire, he agreed to it immediately and helped me with this translated version. His splendid efforts in translation has added more beauty to the chapters. My friend Sumant Dubey has created the cover design poster for the novel.

I am so grateful for having such wonderful friends and family in my life who are as enthusiastic as I am in chasing my dreams.

I sincerely hope that you find this novel as interesting as many of my friends did. I look forward to any feedback that you might have!

K V Raja Saravanan

12-Nov-2020

https://www.facebook.com/raja.saravanan.75

From The Translator's Desk

India's rich cultural heritage is often intertwined with mythology and folklore specific to different regions within its vast lands. It is fascinating to explore these stories that are often hiding in plain sight waiting to be revealed!

The story of Vellaayi was one such that I personally was not aware of - until now. I have thoroughly enjoyed learning more about her, and about Srirangam.

It's been a privilege to be involved in telling this story. I'm so grateful to Raja for taking me along on this journey - and hope you will enjoy it too.

Naveen Ithikkat

12-Nov-2020

Acknowledgments

We wholeheartedly thank our friends and family who always gave constructive feedback as this novel was being developed.

We would like to thank the contributors who made the Tamil version of the novel possible. Thanks to Lakshmi who has edited the Tamil novel, Mary Jane who has painted the scenes of Vellaayi in each of the chapters, Priya who narrated the Tamil Audiobook, Rukmani and Ponraj who proofread the Tamil novel, Rukmani and Srinivas Sampath who have sung in the Tamil audiobook.

We would like to thank our friend Sumant Dubey who has designed the beautiful cover of this novel and also has created the artwork of the world of Vellaayi.

We would like to thank our friend Ashok Natarajan for doing the mixing and mastering of the audiobook tracks of Vellaayi. The English version is currently in the works and we hope to get it out soon.

We would like to thank Mr. Venugopal Lella and his mother Mrs. Santhakumari who helped us with the meaning of the Telugu poems referred to in the novel.

ACKNOWLEDGMENTS

When we were ready to publish the Tamil Novel, we wanted a picture of a dancer on the cover. I had written to Dr. Janaki Rangarajan seeking permission to use her photo to create the cover art form and she readily gave her permission for it. So when we were deciding who should write the foreword for the English Novel, we wanted to have Dr. Janaki Rangarajan to pen it for us. As the novel is based on a female protagonist who is a talented Bharatanatyam dancer, we felt it would be apt to have a foreword written by a talented Bharatanatyam dancer. When we reached out to her with this request, she once again graciously agreed to write the foreword for the novel. Thank you, madam, for your wonderful gesture and also letting us use your photograph to create the cover art for the English novel as well.

The photograph of Namperumal used in this book was taken by R.K. Lakshmi. We thank her for allowing us to use it.

Last but not least we would like our family members who had wholeheartedly supported and encouraged us to create and publish this novel.

Raja Saravanan's family - Wife Rakhi, Parents Kasthuri, Velayutham, Radha, and Rajan

Naveen Ithikkat's family - Wife Jaycy, Kids Riya and Raahil

VELLAAYI

We bow before Lord Namperumal who has blessed us with the opportunity to create this work.

K V Raja Saravanan

Naveen Ithikkat

Date: 12-Nov-2020

Notes on Hindu mythology

This brief section would be useful to readers who may be unfamiliar with aspects of Hindu mythology that are referred to in this novel. For deeper reading on Hindu mythology, there are abundant resources available on the internet.

Hindu mythology has 3 main Gods named Brahma, Vishnu and Shiva. They are referred to as the Hindu Trinity, and represent the cycle of life. Brahma is the creator, Vishnu the preserver, and Shiva the destroyer. Each of the Gods have their own families - who are also worshipped. Of the Trinity, Shiva and Vishnu have two significant sects of worshippers. Those who worshipped Shiva were called Shaivaites and those who worshipped Vishnu were called Vaishnavaites. Both sects had preachers who spread devotion to their respective Gods through poems and stories. The preachers of Shaivism were called Nayanmaars and the preachers of Vaishnavism were called Alwars (Alvars).

Each of the Hindu Gods has many names. Shiva has names like Mahadev, Lingeshwar, Mahesvara, Neelakanta, and many more. Vishnu has names like Narayana, Perumal, Krishna, Vasudeva, and many more.

A temple is a place of worship for Hindus. A single Hindu temple could have shrines (with idols) for many different Hindu gods. Every temple has a 'main' God in the center of the shrine. i.e., a Shiva temple would have Shiva in the center while a Vishnu temple would have Vishnu in the center. The room in the main shrine where the main god idol is located is referred to as sanctum sanctorum. These rooms are usually dark and the idol is made visible by the light from the oil lamps lit near the idol. During festivals, there is a procession that takes place where 'God' is taken around town on a vehicle. Instead of taking out the main idol for such processions, every temple uses a separate procession deity called Urchavar. "Om Namo Narayana" is used as a chant for worshipping Lord Vishnu.

Although numerous temples exist throughout India, some of them assume higher significance due to their deep association with heritage, history, and mythology. This novel is set in the town of Srirangam in Southern India, which is the home to a famous Vishnu temple. There are 108 Vishnu temples (almost all of them in India) that are of special importance, and referred to as 108 Divyadesams. Each Divyadesam has a strong connection to Vishnu mythology. The Vishnu temple in Srirangam is considered to be the first Divyadesam. The

View of Inner Gopurams and Ranga vimaana

Temple Gopurams of Srirangam temple South Entrance

A mandap in the complex of Srirangam Temple

Complex view of Srirangam temple

connection of the temple is to the episode of Ramayana in Hindu mythology. The connection is established in the Prologue chapter. Lord Vishnu is known by the name of Aranganathar or Arangan in Srirangam. The golden tower of the sanctum sanctorum is called Ranga Vimanam. The procession deity of Lord Vishnu in Srirangam goes by the name of Namperumal.

The temple of Srirangam is a large complex. It has entrances from four sides i.e. from the East, West, North, and South respectively. Temple entrances typically have a large tower called *gopuram*. At the Srirangam temple, each *gopuram* has multiple levels, with windows in both directions on each of the levels. On entering through the main entrance, one has to go through seven more doors to reach the main deity in the sanctum sanctorum. In Hindu mythology, this is said to be representative of passing through seven doors in Vishnu's abode in heaven.

As previously mentioned, the saints of Vaishnavism were referred to as Alvars. They have written many poems on Vishnu which are referred to as pasurams. There are many pasurams referred to in this novel. There were twelve Alvars in all. Of the twelve, only one was female - named Andal. Andal's devotion to Lord Vishnu is special, for she considered the Lord to be her love, and was eventually married to Him.

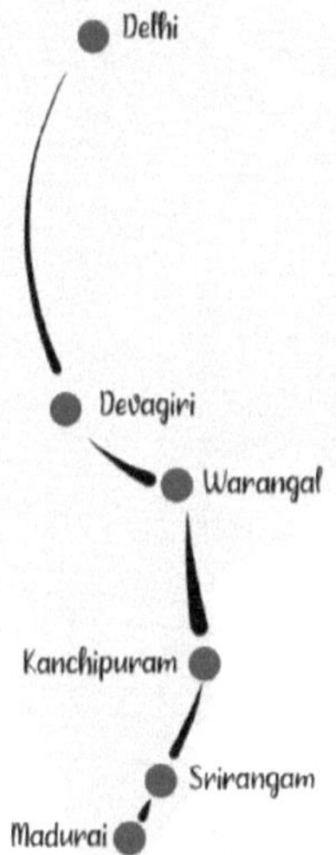

Map of India - 14th Century
depicting the route of Sultnate forces
Delhi
Devagiri
Warangal
Kanchipuram
Srirangam
Madurai

Throughout this book, footnotes have been provided for Indian words, and those have been compiled into a glossary at the end of the book as well.

Happy Reading!

Prologue

Deep within the Brahmagiri Hills nestled in the Kodagu region in the Southern Indian peninsula, a little spring originates. It is joined by other tributaries along its path, and turns into a great river that flows through the Southern states - the Kaveri. She rages through hills and valleys before quieting down somewhat as she reaches Tiruchirappalli. Is she tired from her exhilarating journey, or is she just taking in the gorgeous sights around her? At a place named Mukkombu, the Kollidam river breaks away from the Kaveri. Perhaps because they couldn't say a proper goodbye to one another after such a long journey together, they meet once again – before going their separate ways, this time for good. The beautiful island thus formed is called Srirangam.

This place of unrivalled beauty is the abode of the holy Arangan (i.e., Lord Vishnu). It is said that when Vibhishana was carrying the Grace of Lord Rama aboard the sacred *Ranga Vimana*[1], he decided to stop and rest for a while at Srirangam. However, when it was time to leave, Arangan refused to go along - He seemed to have found His abode.

---

[1] *The shrine over the sanctum sanctorum of the temple at Srirangam.*

Srirangam is the setting of this story.

The story unfolds about 700 years ago from today, a time when the Chola reign had ended, and the Pandya reign was coming to an end as well. Internal power struggles and infighting were the order of the day.

For the benefit of the readers, some background about the geography of Srirangam follows.

Srirangam was (and still is) considered the first of Lord Vishnu's 108 *'Divya Desams'* (or Holy Temples) – as it was the place of the Lord's own choosing. A beautiful city arose around the temple. The city was nourished by the Kaveri to its south, and the Kollidam in the north. The bank along the Kaveri was blanketed by *peepal* and *punnai*[2] trees. To the north of these trees were vast mango groves through which a path had formed. The people of Srirangam would use this path to walk to the Kaveri. One could get to the city of Srirangam by traveling by boat along the Kaveri, and then walking through the mango groves. The southern border was lined with the houses of peasants. Cows were tied in barns behind the homes, while goats and chickens roamed around. On crossing these houses, one could reach the local market – and find shops selling a variety of flowers, fresh fruits and vegetables, elegant clay pots, attractive brass utensils as well as mouth-

---

[2] *Tamil name for Alexandria Laurel trees - evergreen ornamental trees cultivated in tropical areas.*

The World of Vellaayi

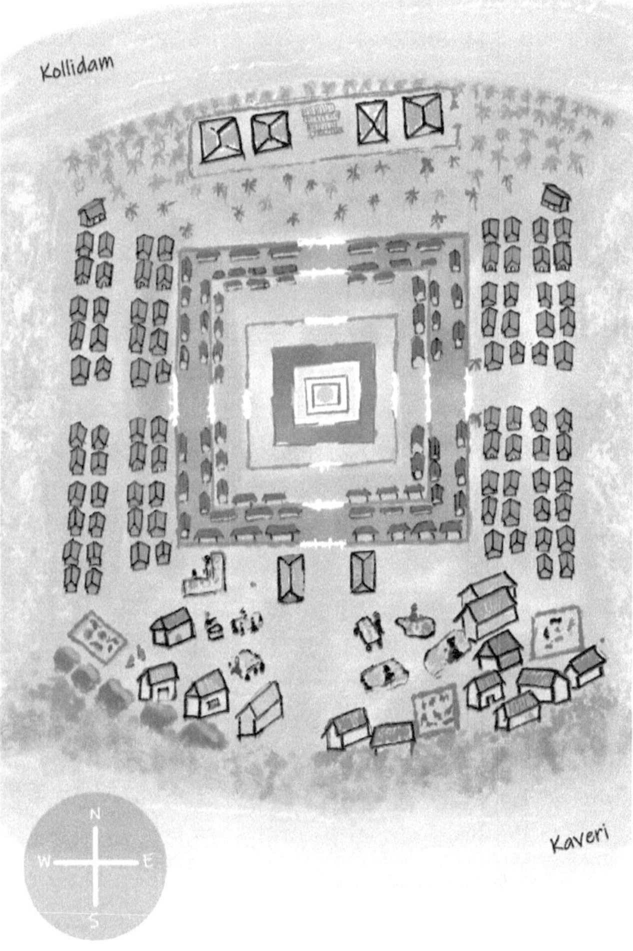

watering sweets. The grand southern tower at the end of the market street would indicate that one had arrived at the temple. It is said that one has to go through seven doors to reach Lord Vishnu's abode in heaven known as Sri Vaikunta. Similarly, there were seven doors in the Srirangam temple to reach the main deity of Lord Vishnu. The main deity is often referred to as Arangan.

The architecture of the temple was in the form of concentric rectangles with doors on each side to enter the inner sanctum sanctorum. The fifth wall opened out to the Uthirai Street. On one side of the street was the wall of the temple, while the other side had a row of houses. Beyond the Uthhirai street was the Chithirai street. This street was constructed to be a little broader so that the chariot carrying the procession deity of Vishnu could be pulled through this street during the Chithirai festival in the month of April. Here there were houses on both sides of the street – which were primarily occupied by devotees and others who worked for the temple. To the north of the temple flowed the Kollidam river – on whose bank grew tall coconut and palm trees. There was also a burial ground on the bank. The temple was flanked by vast fields on the east and west. People would take boats from this beautiful island to travel to places to the south of the Kaveri or to the north of the Kollidam. Fishermen and boatmen lived in huts along the riverbanks.

Now, let's dive into the story!

1. The Child

The morning sky began to glow. A light breeze was blowing. As the first rays of the sun lit up the sky, it felt as though the stars had fallen away into the river and were twinkling with the waves. Birds flew out of their nests in search of food. The sparrows welcomed the sun with their sweet song. Someone else was singing that morning! The sparrows stopped as they heard the enchanting voice of a woman. She was singing Thondaradippodi Alvar's hymn that extolled the Grace of Arangan. In the hymn, the poet exclaims that the experience of basking in the beauty of Arangan could not be traded even for a promise of being in heaven.

Pachai Maamalai Pol Meni

Pavalavai Kamala Chenkan

Achuta Mararere

Aayar Tham Kozhute Ennum

Pachai Maamalai Pol Meni

Pavalvai Kamala Chenkan

Achuta Mararere

Aayar Tham Kozhute Ennum

Echsuvai Thavir Yan Poi

Indiralogam Alum

Achsuvai Perinum Vendean

Arangama Nagarulanea

Those words elevated the beauty of the morning. The singer was a lovely young woman bathing in the river. After she finished her song, she took a final dip in the water, and said a prayer to the Sun. She then did her hair. Her name was Ponni.

As she took in the tranquillity of the morning on the riverbank, she suddenly heard what sounded like a muffled cry. Puzzled, she looked around. Not many others seemed to be on the riverbank that day. There were two others bathing in the river at some distance from her. She heard the cry again, and ran towards a Peepal tree from where the cry seemed to be coming. She looked around and saw a small basket. The basket was intricately woven from bamboo cane. She approached the basket ...and was astounded by what she saw inside – a beautiful baby girl draped in a red silk cloth with a golden yellow

border. On seeing Ponni, the little child giggled with laughter. Ponni was stunned.

Ponni was from a family of *'devadasis'* – generations of women who considered themselves 'wedded' to Arangan, and who sang and danced in the temple in His praise. There were two kinds of devadasis. There were those who engaged in relationships with men and dedicated their children to the service of the Lord, and then there were those who were celibate and utterly devoted themselves to the Lord. Ponni was of the second kind. Denying her inner longing for someone to call her own, she zealously directed all her affections to the service of Arangan. Now this child, this beautiful child, her voice, her laughter, all evoked all of Ponni's maternal instincts. The trees rustled in a strong gust of wind. The waters of the Kaveri gently lapped against the banks. Ponni woke from her stupor. She looked around her. There was no-one – nobody to even ask "Is this your child?".

She sat down near the child and took her in her arms. She lovingly embraced her and kissed her on the forehead. She felt as though she were holding a beautiful lotus flower. She felt that the poet Kalidas would need to be reborn so that the beauty of the child could be adequately described! The baby's soft silky hair, the eyes that resembled black beetles, the mouth that babbled, the gorgeous dimples on the cheeks, the fingers like sunflower petals, the feet like deep red lotuses, all these mesmerized Ponni. She repeatedly kissed the baby on the forehead, cheeks, palms and feet. She sat there for a while. When anyone passed, she feared that it might be someone to claim the baby. However, an hour passed, and no one came. She thought that the Lord himself had seen her inner desire and granted her this child. The prayer bell rang in the temple. Ponni started to walk towards her home carrying the child.

Ponni walked by the southern Uthhirai street and arrived at the entrance to the East Tower. This entrance faced the feet of the Arangan lying down in the *Ananthasayanam*[3] pose. As promised to Vibheeshana, the Arangan was lying down facing Sri Lanka in the south. Thus, His feet were facing east. Ponni visualized the child embracing the Lord's feet and prayed for her to be blessed. The rays of the morning sun sparkled on the 'kalasam's (i.e. inverted pot-shaped tips) of the temple towers. The child clapped and giggled when she glimpsed this. Ponni lovingly looked at the baby – whose body seemed to glow as the sun's rays fell on her.

Ponni named the child 'Vellai Ammal' (i.e. The Fair One). "Such a suitable name!" – she thought to herself and beamed. When she playfully babbled with the child, pinched her cheek and called her 'Vellaayi', the baby giggled again.

---

[3] *Literally meaning "sleeping on the serpent named Ananta (infinity)", it is a symbolic representation of the cosmic balance of finity within infinity.*

2. Aadi Perukku

"Vellaayi!", Ponni called out as Vellaayi, now seven years old, played in the verandah.

"Yes, Amma!", Vellaayi responded, and came running into the house.

"I just made a garland of flowers. Could you take it to the priest at the temple and come back?", Ponni asked.

"Sure, Amma!", said Vellaayi as she jumped happily and picked up the basket containing the garland. She set off towards the temple as fast as her little feet could take her.

"Vellaayi! Don't sit there too long listening to the priest's stories. Come back soon!" - said Ponni - but her words barely made their way to Vellaayi's ears.

The priest whom Vellaayi was eager to meet was the priest of the *Andal*[4] shrine in the temple. His name was Thiruvengadam, and he was about sixty years old. Vellaayi lovingly referred to him as "Grandpa". Thiruvengadam performed rituals at the *Andal* shrine, which was near the east entrance of the temple. He

---

[4] *The only female Alvar among the 12 Alvar saints of South India. The Alvar saints are known for their affiliation to the Vaishnava tradition of Hinduism.*

was unmarried. He was utterly devoted to Andal. He sported the tridental mark of Vishnu - the *Thirunamam* - on his forehead. He had a gentle demeanor and a deep baritone voice. He was popular with the regular visitors of the temple, who always stopped by to have a chat with him and hear his soothing words. After performing the worship rituals in the shrine, he would sing *pasurams* (i.e. hymn about Lord Vishnu) written by Andal. Later he would recite stories of Andal's love for Lord Vishnu. Vellaayi just loved those stories. Even though she had heard the stories many times before, she would still listen to them every time as if it were the first time. Thiruvengadam also adored Vellaayi. "If I'd had a family, and a grandchild, she would have been like Vellaayi.", he would sometimes think to himself.

Vellaayi reached the Andal shrine carrying the flower basket. She reached just as Thiruvengadam started to sing the *pasuram* written by Andal. The *pasuram* was about a dream of Andal's, in which the Lord had come with an entourage of a thousand elephants to ask for her hand in marriage. In the *pasuram*, Andal was describing her dream to her friends. Vellaayi quickly kept the basket down and started to dance to the song.

Vaaranam aayiram soozha valam seidhu ,

Naarana Nambi nadakkindraan yendredhir,

Poorana pokudam vaithu , puramengum ,

Thoranam naatta kana kanden thozhi , naan.

...

Maddalam kotta vari sangam nindru oodha ,

Muthudai thamam   nirai thaazhntha pandhar keezh,

Maithunan nambi madhu soodanan vandhu   yennai,

Kaithalam paththa kanaa kanden thozhi, naan.

Thiruvengadam sang all of ten *pasurams* that described the events leading up to the grand marriage event. Vellaayi danced to the 'beats' that Thiruvengadam created by tapping his hands on his thighs as he sang. Her beautiful eyes, expressive hands, and energetic feet brought the *pasurams* to life. The temple was busier than usual due to the festival of *Aadiperukku*[5], and the combination of Thiruvengadam's soulful voice and Vellaayi's exquisite dancing attracted a large crowd to the shrine. Vellaayi finished her dance with the portrayal of the scene where Kodhai (which is another name for Andal) and Vishnu went around the town on an elephant after their marriage. The crowd gave a big round of applause.

---

[5] *Aadi is the fourth month of the Tamil Calendar, which marks the onset of monsoons. Aadi Perukku denotes the floods in the river due to the monsoons in the month of Aadi.*

"How beautifully that child danced! It was like we were watching Kodhai's marriage with our own eyes!", many in the crowd praised as they dispersed. Thiruvengadam put the garland on Andal's statue inside the shrine, and performed the worship rituals. He took the *aarti*[6] towards Vellaayi. She placed her hands over the *aarti* and then over her eyes. After Thiruvengadam took some *kumkum*[7] and applied it on her forehead, she prostrated before him. Thiruvengadam asked her to get up, placed the *aarti* plate down and sat near a pillar. Vellaayi sat next to him.

"Kodhai! You dance so well, ask your mother to ward off any evil eye that might be cast on you", said Thiruvengadam as he patted the back of her head. He often called her Kodhai. As Periyalzhwar was proud of his daughter Kodhai (another name for Andal), Thiruvengadam's heart also filled with pride as he saw Vellaayi grow up.

"Grandpa, is there a special festival today?",asked Vellaayi.

"Yes Kodhai, today is Aadiperukku."

"What does that mean?"

---

[6] *A Hindu religious ritual of worship, in which light is offered to one or more deities.*
[7] *A red powder, made from saffron or turmeric, used ceremonially by Hindu women to make various markings on the body.*

Namperumal

"Every year, on the 18th day of the month of *Aadi*, the Kaveri swells up, marking the onset of the monsoon season. It is truly a sight to behold! That is when the marriage of the Lord to Kaveri's daughter is celebrated. Today Namperumal will be present in the *mandap*[8] on the banks of Kaveri. In the evening there will be a ritual wherein we offer gifts to Kaveri, and ask for her daughter's hand for the Lord in return."

Namperumal is the procession deity of the Srirangam temple. Every temple would have the main deity in the sanctum sanctorum of the temple. There would be a separate procession deity that would be taken around the temple during festival processions.

"Shall we also go, Grandpa?", asked Vellaayi excitedly.

"Your mother told me that she wasn't able to attend the festival the last two years as she was busy with dance programs, but that she would definitely come this year. You could join her when she comes."

"Oh, is that so? I'll come for sure, Grandpa!", Vellaayi said as she turned and ran home.

In the evening, many people gathered near the *mandap* (known today as "Amma Mandapam") on the banks of the Kaveri and prayed for Namperumal's blessings. There were residents of Srirangam, as well as those who had come from many other places. Many sat under trees in groups, and ate the sweets and

---

[8] *A covered structure with pillars.*

savories that they had brought with them. Others enjoyed popped rice balls, groundnuts, and *adhirasam*[9]. Some groups got together and sang bhajans about Lord Narayana. Others sang along. Children played on the bank of the river, building sandcastles. The elders kept an eye on them so that they didn't run into the Kaveri - which was filled to the brim.

Ponni and Vellaayi arrived. Vellaayi was awestruck looking at Namperumal. He was aglow in a golden hue, sporting a turban embedded with precious stones on his head, adorning golden necklaces around his neck, and dressed in a blue-colored silk robe with a golden border. He sat under a golden umbrella. He looked like an immaculately-dressed bridegroom. Vellaayi hadn't seen such a beautiful version of Namperumal before. She refused to budge despite her mother asking her to move along. She was transfixed by Namperumal. She felt as though Namperumal had dressed up for her. Close to where Namperumal was placed, stood an aged and charismatic-looking person, donning a saffron robe and the tridental mark of Vishnu on his forehead. He carefully watched over the proceedings. It was Pillai Lokacharyar, who was supervising the prayers and rituals at the Srirangam temple. Everything that happened there was as per his advice and guidance. Two of his disciples stood beside him helping with the proceedings.

---

[9] *A type of Indian sweet.*

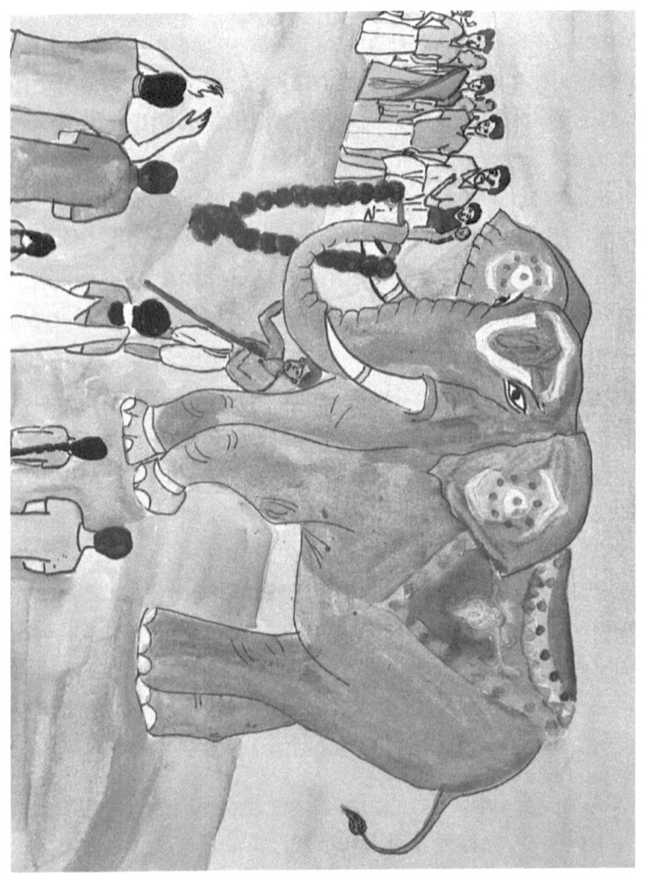

At that moment, there was a thunderous sound that seemed to silence everything else around. Two people shouted "Please give way, Please give way!" as they walked towards Namperumal. The crowd split, and a path was created in between. As the path cleared, the source of that sound also came into sight. Gajendran the elephant stood there majestically. (As mentioned in the *'Gajendra Moksham'*, Lord Vishnu had once rescued an elephant named Gajendran from peril. Since then, over many generations, a lineage of elephants have served the Lord. Every elephant in that lineage was called Gajendran.) Gajendran started to walk down the path that was created. Vellaayi looked at him curiously. As the elephant walked up to Namperumal, it bent on its knees to pray to the Lord. When he got up, Pillai Lokacharyar presented him with a plate on which a garland was placed. Gajendran picked up the garland with his trunk and raised it high. Everyone in the crowd chanted "Om Namo Narayanaya". Gajendran turned around and walked towards the river. The two men now split the crowd to create a path to the river. As Gajendran neared the river, he threw the garland into it. Everyone around applauded, chanting "Om Namo Narayanaya".

"Amma, why did Gajendran throw the garland into the river?", asked Vellaayi.

"It did not throw the garland dear.", Ponni smiled at her daughter's innocent question. "It is a gift offered to Kaveri, asking for her daughter's hand for the Lord". Vellaayi turned around. People were offering flowers and fruits to Kaveri.

"You stay here, dear. I will also offer some flowers to Kaveri and come back.", said Ponni as she walked towards the river leaving Vellaayi behind. There was a *champak*[10] tree where Vellaayi stood. A *champak* flower fell on her from the tree. She picked it up and looked at it for a while. She then started to walk towards the river that was now raging with full force. Everyone was so involved with making their offerings to the river that they did not notice a child walk toward the river. Vellaayi reached the bank, and threw the flower in. The monsoon wind pushed it back towards Vellaayi before it could fall into the river. She walked a couple of feet towards the river and picked up the flower. Thinking that the wind might blow her flower back to the shore again if she threw it, she made sure to walk up to the river so that her feet touched the water. She then bent down slowly, and placed the flower onto the water. It floated away gently. To make it move faster she started pushing the water. The flower danced ahead a little. Totally immersed in the moment, she walked a few more feet into the river without even realizing it.

"Oh! There is a child alone in the river!", someone shouted from the crowd. Ponni turned toward the

---

[10] *Magnolia champaca, an evergreen tree known for its fragrant flowers.*

direction of the sound - and was terrified by what she saw.

"Vellaayi! Don't go further! Come back to the shore!", she screamed as she ran towards her. Vellaayi lifted her head up to look at her mother. She tried to walk towards her, but her legs wouldn't move. Instead, she felt herself drifting away from her mother.

"Amma! Amma!", she cried, but to no avail. She was already neck-deep in water. Her feet couldn't hold on to the shore anymore. In seconds, her mother's face faded away, and darkness engulfed her.

3. Paavai Nonbu

It was getting harder to breathe. Vellaayi felt as if she was traveling through an infinite space. She felt increasingly drowsy, as a sense of numbness spread through her body. Suddenly, a light broke through the darkness, and seemed to be coming towards her. It grew into a massive flame of light. Vellaayi opened her eyes wide. Her breathing steadied. She wasn't struggling in the water anymore - it felt like she was floating now. It seemed as if she were being pulled towards the flame. The light from the flame shone on her face. What she saw gave her goosebumps. Namperumal stood within the ball of flame, dressed in a groom's attire. He smiled gently at Vellaayi. He had a garland in his hand. Vellaayi quickly recognized that it was the same garland that Gajendran had offered to the river. He threw the garland towards Vellaayi, and she grasped it firmly. Namperumal pulled her towards him. The light was blinding. Vellaayi closed her eyes. Namperumal took some water in his hand and sprinkled it over her face. As the water sprinkled over her eyes, her eyelids fluttered like a butterfly's wings. She opened her eyes slowly and saw the Golden statue of Namperumal. She looked around but couldn't see the flame of light anymore. The darkness was replaced by the light from the rays of the setting sun. The deafening silence was replaced by the sounds from a crowd of people. She realized that she was lying down on the floor of the *mandap* where the deity of Namperumal was kept.

Pillai Lokacharyar was looking down at her holding a small brass vessel filled with holy water. Thiruvengadam was standing behind him. Relief was writ large on his face.

"Dear child, don't fear. You are safe.", said Pillai Lokacharyar with a warm smile.

Ponni immediately hugged her tightly and said, "Oh dear Vellaayi, I thought I had lost you. The good Lord saved you. He sent Kannan to save you at the right time". That's when Vellaayi noticed another man standing near her mother. He had a dhoti tied around his waist. His dark-complexioned body was still drenched in water. It was the boatman Kannan.

Ponni noticed Vellaayi's puzzled look and said, "When you had drowned in the river, I had lost all hope. Luckily Kannan was there at that time. He was there to pull his boats to the shore to prevent them from being washed away in the floods. But when he saw you drowning, he jumped into the river and saved you. Acharyaar sprinkled holy water on you to bring you back to consciousness. That's when you opened your eyes".

Kannan smiled at Vellaayi. The crowd slowly dispersed. But Vellaayi was confused. She didn't know what was true - what she had seen, or what her mother was saying. She looked at the deity of

Namperumal, and felt like He was gently smiling at her. She couldn't hold back her tears. This incident greatly impacted Vellaayi. Her love for Namperumal grew manifold. She started to believe that like Kodhai, she was also born to be united with Namperumal.

Four years had passed since that incident. It was the day after the monsoon season had ended. The waters of the Kaveri river had calmed. In the clear sky in the month of *Margazhi*[11], the full moon shone brightly. The gentle cold breeze sweeping over the Kaveri river seemed to be giving her the shivers, making her break into 'goosebumps' in the form of small waves. It was about an hour before sunrise. The full moon bid goodbye to his friends - the trees, the creepers, the river - with whom he had played all night, by hugging them with his silver arms. The silence was broken by laughter from a group of young girls. The group was walking towards the Kaveri. Vellaayi walked in front of the group. She was 11 years old now. Her beauty had also grown, and it seemed to compete with the beauty of the full moon that day. The scene of her walking with her friends was akin to a visual of the full moon sailing amidst a group of stars. Unperturbed by the chilly weather, all of them took a bath in the river. Later they got on to the *mandap*, dried their hair and sung the *pasurams* from

---

[11] *The ninth month of the Tamil Calendar, which has more festivals and events than other months.*

Thirupaavai[12] literature written by Andal. Vellaayi rubbed a piece of sandalwood on the floor with water, took the paste and applied it to her forehead. She then broke into a dance to a song that her friends sang. A few of her friends danced along. As she danced, the water that dripped from her clothes formed beautiful art on the floor of the *mandap*.

Maargazhith thingal madhi niraindha nannaalaal

neeraadap podhuveer podhumino nerizhaiyeer

seer malgum aayppaadic celvac cirumeergaal

koorver kodunthozhilan nandhagopan kumaran

Eraarndha kanni yasodhai ilanysingam

kaar menic cengan kadhir madhiyam pol mugaththhaan

naaraayanane namakke parai tharuvaan

paaror pugazhap padindhelor embaavaay

To understand the reason behind what appears to be a silly thing to do on a cold winter morning, it might be useful to understand the background. Andal, in the

---

[12] *Tamil devotional poem by Andal. It is a part of the Divya Prabandha, a collection of the works of the twelve Alvars, that is considered an important part of the devotional genre of Tamil literature.*

first *pasuram* she had written in Thiruppaavai, calls out to young virgin girls to bathe while the moon is still in the sky and pray to Lord Krishna. She asks them to perform this for all of the month of *Margazhi*, in order to find a husband who had the qualities of Lord Krishna. This ritual is called *"Paavai Nonbu"* in Tamil Nadu. Vellaayi and her friends were celebrating this ritual with a lot of enthusiasm and fun. The sun rose in the east as if he wanted to enjoy the song and dance. As the rays filled the *mandap*, the girls finished singing and dancing for the thirtieth *pasuram* from *Thirupaavai*. As Vellaayi concluded her dance for the last line of the *pasuram* which said that "those who sing these thirty *pasurams* would have the blessings of the Lord Vishnu", the golden rays of the rising sun embraced her and enhanced her beauty.

Vellaayi and her friends then took the path leading from the river through the mango groves into town. The morning sun had risen, and made the surroundings look much brighter than how it was when they had walked towards the river earlier in the morning. A young man on a horse was advancing towards them. The very sight of him filled Vellaayi with disgust, and her feelings were more than apparent on her face. It was Bhoopathi - the son of a goldsmith in Uraiyur. He was attracted to Vellaayi ever since he saw her dance at the Vishnu temple in Uraiyur a month prior. Since that day, whenever he met her, he would mouth romantic lines at her, which she abhorred. As he reached near them, he stopped his horse in their path, blocking their way. Vellaayi glared at him furiously.

"Oh, I had come here to witness your dance, but missed it Vellaayi! Could you dance once more for me?", he asked in a tone that Vellaayi always found disgusting.

"Why should I dance for you?", snapped Vellaayi.

"You know, you look so beautiful even when you are angry. I could adorn you with gold and enhance your beauty.", he said.

"You can hold onto your gold. My dance and singing belong to my Lord Namperumal. Your gold is worthless before Him."

"Oh, so that's what it is. If you like that statue made of *Abaranji*[13] gold, I could make you jewels made of *Abaranji* gold worth much more than Namperumal."

Vellaayi seethed when she heard him refer to Namperumal as a statue. She felt like tearing him to pieces.

"For a fool like you, mere gold seems to be worth more than the priceless blessings of the Lord", said Vellaayi as she pushed the horse forcefully. The horse ran a few steps away from the spot before Bhoopathi could stop it. He was surprised that a young girl like her had the strength to push the horse aside.

---

[13] *'purest' gold*

"I will come back to you one day to learn about the significance of the Lord's blessings!", he shouted at her.

Vellaayi and her friends Ignored his words and walked ahead quickly. After they crossed the mango groves, they passed by a row of houses. As they were going through the Chithirai street, they saw that the front yards of the houses had beautiful *rangoli*[14]s drawn with rice powder. Vellaayi's anger dissolved as she looked at the beautiful patterns. She and her friends took some time to appreciate the beauty of each one of the *rangolis*. Once they reached their homes, they changed and left for the temple.

Inside the temple premises, a large crowd had gathered in the *mandap* outside the innermost complex where Lord Arangan was situated. The crowd seemed to be listening to something eagerly. Vellaayi and her friends were curious to know what was happening, so they went into the crowd to see for themselves. Pillai Lokacharyar was sitting in the center of the *mandap*. His disciples stood beside him. Thiruvengadam stood near the pillar behind Pillai Lokacharyar. There was a person seated opposite Pillai Lokacharyar. He was dressed in a silk shirt, silk dhoti, and silk *angavasthiram*[15]. He had Vishnu's tridential

---

[14] *Indian art form, in which patterns are created on the floor or the ground using materials such as coloured rice, coloured sand, quartz powder or flower petals.*

[15] *Traditional rectangular white piece of cloth or stole, worn by men from the Hindu community, which is draped over the shoulders.*

mark on his forehead. He had some palm leaf manuscripts in his hand. He read them for a while. Then he kept the manuscripts aside and closed his eyes as if immersed in deep thought. Every eye in the crowd was focused on him - expecting him to say something.

The person was Vishnudasan, an astrologer from Uraiyur. He was well-known in the nearby towns for his predictions. Before the full moon night ended in *Margazhi*, he looked at the horizon to predict the monsoon in the upcoming year. In those days, monsoons were predicted by the colour of the sky around the horizon - a greyish hue would indicate the arrival of a good monsoon, whereas a reddish hue would indicate a bad one. Good astrologers could make fairly accurate predictions based on this phenomenon and share it with people. Based on the prediction, farmers would decide on the crops for the season. Besides predicting rainfall, the astrologers also made predictions about the prosperity of the town. This crowd had gathered here to listen to the predictions for the year. Vishnudasan opened his eyes. The wrinkles on his forehead foretold his worrisome thoughts.

Pillai Lokacharyar noticed this and asked, "Vishnudasa, what is the matter? You look worried. Would there be any problem with the rainfall this year?"

"Acharya, there is no such issue. Today the horizon is draped in a silver hue - there will be very good rainfall this monsoon. The Kaveri will likely overflow this year", Vishnudasan said.

There was jubilation when the crowd heard this. Some of them looked towards the sanctum sanctorum of the Lord and shouted, "Om Namo Narayanaya!"

Pillai Lokacharyar looked at Vishnudasan, whose face now showed deep worry.

"A good amount of rainfall is news to rejoice. But why do you look so worried?"

"Yes Acharya, that is news to rejoice, but...", he paused.

"What?"

"As per my predictions, Srirangam is entering an extraordinarily difficult phase. The coming years will bring a great deal of sorrow.", he said with hesitation.

Silence engulfed the crowd. Pillai Lokacharyar broke the silence and spoke, "The Lord himself has chosen this town as his abode. He will save the town from any kind of trouble."

Shouts of "Yes...Yes!" echoed in the crowd in agreement with what Pillai Lokacharyar had said.

"It is in fact... a troublesome period for.... the Lord himself.", said Vishnudasan hesitatingly.

"What are you saying?", asked Pillai Lokacharyar, shocked.

"There will be many obstacles in the worship rituals performed for the Lord. The next twelve years will be very hard. Many lives will be lost as well.", said Vishnudasan.

The crowd gasped. Pillai Lokacharyar closed his eyes and prayed to the Lord. Then he opened his eyes and spoke - "The Lord has taken care of us for all these years and blessed us abundantly. The hardship we are about to endure is not permanent. He will lead us through the dark times. We should all be in this together to ensure there is no ill-effect on the Lord Himself. It is our duty to protect Him. For this too, He will guide us. All of you, pray to the Lord to give you the strength to face this difficult time. Om Namo Narayanaya!" He stood up as he said those words.

"Om Namo Narayanaya", the chant from the crowd echoed around the temple walls and filled the air in Srirangam.

From the time Vellaayi heard the prediction, she felt extremely uneasy. She seemed to be able to think only about the perils that loomed. She told her mother Ponni about what she heard at the temple.

"The Lord who has saved us from all perils thus far would help us with this too. Don't worry my child", said Ponni.

That night Vellaayi couldn't sleep for a long time. When she finally fell asleep after midnight, she had a dream. On a full moon night, she was standing atop the highest storey of the eastern *gopuram*[16] of the temple. The *Ranga Vimana* shone brightly reflecting the rays from the full moon. She folded her hands together in a *namaskaram*[17], looking at it with tear-filled eyes. "Kodhai", she heard someone calling out for her and turned around. She saw Namperumal standing there. He was in the attire of a bridegroom, just as she had seen Him when she had drowned in the river.

"My Lord", she said brimming with emotion.

"It is a difficult time for me. You need to help me", said Namperumal.

As she heard these words Vellaayi prostrated before Him.

"What are you saying, my Lord? You are the One who saves the world, how can I save You?", she asked.

When there was no response, she raised her head to look at Him. But He was not there anymore. Vellaayi woke up in a state of shock.

---

[16] *Monumental entrance tower, usually ornate, at the entrance of a Hindu temple in Southern India.*

[17] *Namaste / namaskar / namaskaram is a customary, non-contact form of Hindu greeting.*

4. Malik Kafur

A hurricane takes its time to form. Water droplets from the sea vaporize and rise to form clouds. Aided by warm air and gusting winds, these clouds gather speed, turning into a hurricane.

Likewise, there was an event about two centuries ago in India, that foreshadowed a troublesome period for the country. In the year 1001 AD, Mahmud Ghazni came with his forces from the west to conquer India. His methods of war caught the Indian rulers by surprise. Although he lost a battle in the beginning, he persisted, and in due course, captured a few kingdoms in North India - but that was just the beginning. More forces from the west came into India, and conquered many more territories. One such conquest made Jalaluddin the King of Delhi in the year 1290 AD. His son-in-law Alauddin Khalji led the forces to many wars and won. Once he conquered Devagiri (known as Daulatabad in the present day), he became greedier. He killed his father-in-law Jalaluddin and was crowned the King of Delhi in 1296 AD. Stories of his conquests struck terror in the hearts of people in South India as well. He took many slaves when he conquered the lands of Gujarat. He was particularly impressed by the bravery of one of the slaves. He converted him to his religion and rechristened him as Malik Kafur.

Malik Kafur fought many wars for Alauddin Khalji. In 1310 AD he started marching with his army towards the South. The fact that the king of Warangal, Prathapa Rudra had gone away to fight the Pandyas made his job easier. He easily took over the city of Warangal and by extension, most of its wealth. This left no option for the King Prathapa Rudra but to surrender. This victory further emboldened Malik Kafur. He took the help of Prathapa Rudra to wage war against the Pandyas. His army won battles against all the Pandyan feudatories and plundered most of their wealth as they proceeded further. The riches that kings had handed over to temples now became part of his booty.

Adjacent to the northern boundary of Tiruchirapalli, there is a small town called Thiruvellarai. This is also part of the 108 *Divya Desams* of the Lord Vishnu. The main deity of the Lord Vishnu is named as *Pundarikakshan* in this temple. The *pasurams* that were written between 600 AD and 900 AD refer to this temple. The term *Vellarai* means white colored rock. The history of the temple dates back to the *Treta Yuga*[18]. The temple is said to be built by the legendary King Sibi. Once when King Sibi had come with his forces to Thiruvellarai, a white boar was spotted. The soldiers tried to hunt it down, but their efforts were in vain. Seeing this, the King himself went

---

[18] *The second of the four Yugas, or ages of mankind, in Hinduism.*

to hunt it down. But the white boar seemed to disappear into a hole in the ground. King Sibi was surprised by what he saw. A sage by the name Markendeya happened to be in penance there. The King approached him and asked him about the incident he had witnessed. Markendeya said that it was Lord Vishnu who was in the form of the boar. He asked the King to worship the boar by offering milk through the hole in which it had disappeared. The King followed the advice given by the sage and worshipped the Lord. Lord Vishnu appeared before him. He asked him to build a temple at the location by employing 3700 Vaishanvites. The King gathered 3700 Vaishnavites and started to build a temple at the location. But one of the Vaishnavite died during the process. When the team was unable to proceed further due to this, the Lord himself came in the form of a Vaishnavite called *Pundarikakshan* and helped in the completion of the temple. So goes the history of the temple.

Arinodoru nangudai nedumudiyarakkanran
siramellaam veru

vrruga villadu valaittavane enakkarul puriye

maaril sodiya maragadap paasadai tamaraimalar
vaartta

teral mandi vandinnisai mural tiruvellarai ninraane

Thirumangai Azhwar had written this *pasuram* on this temple. In this *pasuram*, he asks the Lord who had killed the ten-headed demon to bless him. He describes the Lord as being seated in the Thiruvellarai temple that is surrounded by ponds filled with water, holding beautiful Lotus flowers around which many bees hummed.

The place that was once filled with Lotus flowers and humming bees, now resembled a desert where vultures circled the air. In the forest clearing towards the South of the temple, a tent was pitched in. A battalion of soldiers sat around the tent. Horses were tied to the trees around the tent. A few of the men cooked meat over a fire. The smoke from the fire raised the already hot temperature that May. The soldiers did not belong to the area. They looked like an army that had traveled far. Amidst the crowd, a man sat on a rock beside the tent. More than 6 feet tall, he wore a dress that looked like the war suit of the army from the west that now ruled North India. He wore a black turban, and held a sword in his hand. The tip of the sword touched the ground, and the bloodstain on it reflected in his eyes, making him look terrifying. It was Malik Kafur. His army of men had looted all the wealth from the Thiruvellarai temple and had killed anyone who stood in their way. In the olden days, the kings built humble palaces for themselves and donated a great deal of wealth to the temples to build golden roofs for the Lord. Malik Kafur's army took advantage of this. They looted many temples and thus acquired a large amount of wealth.

Two soldiers held a young man tied by a rope and brought him to Malik Kafur. The young man was Bhoopathi, the son of a goldsmith in Uraiyur.

"Captain, we found him on the bank of the Kollidam. He saw us and tried to escape. We caught him, and found that he was carrying a lot of gold. We immediately brought him here", said one of them.

Malik Kafur's reddish eyes filled with excitement when he heard 'gold'. He eyed Bhoopathi carefully.

"Who are you? How come you have so much gold on you?", he asked harshly.

"Sir, I am the son of a goldsmith from Uraiyur. I buy and sell gold in and around this area", Bhoopathi said.

"Oh, is that so? Capturing you is akin to finding a treasure!", he said and laughed aloud. Everyone around him joined him in the laughter - which echoed like thunder for a few moments.

"Sir, please return my gold. I would be very grateful.", Bhoopathi said.

"Who needs your gratitude?"

"My loyalty will benefit you many times over."

"How?"

"I can show you a place that has far more treasures than the gold that I have now."

"Treasure of gold? Where is it?", asked Malik Kafur greedily.

"Srirangam! The place that houses Namperumal, made of *Abaranji* gold", Bhoopathi said.

Malik Kafur's eyes widened. There was a smirk on his face. The next morning his army started to march towards Srirangam.

Meanwhile, inside the Srirangam temple, Vellaayi was listening to stories from Thiruvengadam as they were seated in the *mandap* of the Andal shrine.

"Grandpa, during the Chithirai festival, there are a lot of gold jewels on Namperumal. Who gave all this gold?", asked Vellaayi.

Thiruvengadam smiled. He always had interesting stories for the questions Vellaayi asked him.

"Over the years, as this blessed land was ruled by the Pallavas, the Chozhas and then the Pandyas, they all gave this temple a great deal of wealth from their spoils of war. In particular, Sadayavarman Sundarapandian who rose to the throne after Maravarman Sundarapandian, performed a *Gaja Thulabharam* to donate the wealth he had accumulated from his victories to the temple. Those jewels adorn the Lord during festivities", he said.

"*Gaja Thulabharam*? What is that Grandpa?", asked Vellaayi.

"Our Pandya King Sadayavarman Sundarapandian won the battle for the fort of Kannanur against the Hoysala King Veerasomeswaran. He won a lot of wealth in terms of gold, horses, and elephants. He distributed that wealth among temples. For his donations to our Srirangam temple, he conducted a new *Thulabharam*[19]. He let two boats float on the Kaveri river. He got onto one of the boats seated on his royal elephant, he then had the other boat filled with gold and ornaments such that it equaled the weight of the boat on which he was seated on his royal elephant. He donated all the gold and ornaments to Arangan. This is the story of Gaja Thulabharam", said Thiruvegadam.

Vellaayi listened to the story with awe. Before they could start the next conversation, boatman Kannan ran inside the temple. As he saw them first he ran towards them.

"Where is Acharya?", he asked, gasping for breath.

"He should be in the main sanctum sanctorum", Thiruvengadam replied.

"By the way Kanna, what happened?..." Before Thiruvengadam could complete, Kannan ran towards the sanctum sanctorum. Thiruvengadam sensed that something untoward had happened and ran behind him. Vellaayi too followed suit.

As they reached near the inner shrine, Pillai Lokacharyar came out.

---

[19] *An ancient Hindu practice in which a person is weighed against a commodity (such as gold, grain, fruits or other objects), and the equivalent weight of that commodity is offered as donation to a temple.*

"Acharya, we are in danger… grave danger!", said Kannan, sounding terrified.

Pillai Lokacharyar was calm and poised. He asked calmly, "Tell me slowly Kanna, what sort of danger?"

"A group of dacoits from North India is marching towards Srirangam. They are on the northern bank of the Kollidam river. They could be here within an hour. A boatman from the Kollidam river told me", he said.

Thiruvengadam and Vellaayi were shocked. Although Pillai Lokacharyar was shaken, he did not show it.

"Om Namo Narayana", he chanted and sank into deep thought. He looked at the sky, where dark clouds lurked.

"There is no time to think or debate over what needs to be done. We should save the temple and Namperumal. Arangan will guide us.", he said, and looked at Kannan.

"Kanna, will you do what I say without questioning my intent?", he asked Kannan.

"Acharya, please tell me, I will do it.", he said.

"Go immediately to the *mandap* on the bank of the Kaveri. Wait there for an hour and a half. Then tell the boatmen and their families living there that heavy rains and flooding is imminent in the Kaveri. Ask them to bring their belongings to the temple and stay here.

Tell them that I have asked them to do so.", Pillai Lokacharyar said.

"But...?", Kannan started to ask, but then thought to himself that the *Achuryar*[20] must have a good reason for saying what he did. He promptly set off towards the Kaveri.

Once he left, Pillai Lokacharyar went inside the shrine along with Thiruvengadam and Vellaayi. He asked his disciples Rangachari and Srinivasan to join him. He looked at Lord Vishnu in the *Ananthasayanam* pose inside the sanctum sanctorum. He closed his eyes and prayed to the Lord. He then asked Rangachari and Srinivasan to bring the two wooden caskets covered in silk cloth that were kept in a corner of the shrine. Then with the help of Rangachari and Srinivasan, he placed the procession deities of Namperumal and Ranganayaki into each of them. They closed the caskets, and covered them back with the silk cloth.

"Thiruvengadam, you take this casket that has Namperumal to your house and keep it safe. Ask some of the women and children in the town to hide inside your house. As your house is at the east end of the town, it will be a while before the dacoits get there. By then, hopefully, we would have a plan to handle this threat", he said.

He then turned towards Srinivasan.

---

[20] *Expert instructor in matters such as religion, or any other subject.*

"Srinivasa, you can keep Ranganayaki in your house which is at the west end of the town. Also, have the remaining women and children in the town hide in your house.", he said without pause.

Everyone hesitated.

"There is no time to think. Please keep your faith in the Lord Arangan and move quickly.", he said.

Thiruvengadam and Vellaayi carried Namperumal along with them. As Thiruvengadam went to his house, Vellaayi gathered her mother Ponni and some of the women and children in the town. All of them proceeded to Thiruvengadam's house. By the time they reached the house, Thiruvengadam had made all the required arrangements. The room at the far end of the house had a room with a large circular earthen pot for storing grains. He asked everyone to go into that room.

"No matter what you hear outside, do not step out. The Lord Arangan will save us.", he said and then locked the door from the outside.

The remaining women and children hid in Srinivasan' house. Meanwhile, Pillai Lokacharyar, with the help of another disciple Rangachari and some temple priests, divided the jewels and gold coins of the temple into two equal parts and put them into two large wooden boxes. Rangachari and the priests took one of the boxes near the main deity in the sanctum sanctorum. Pillai Lokacharyar went behind the deity and sat on the floor. He pressed a stone slab on the floor. It moved slightly. Then, as per his instructions, two men moved the slab that moved. There was a room hidden below the slab. They kept one of the wooden boxes inside it and closed the room with the stone slab. Then they took the other box to the well that was near the Andal shrine. They lowered the box into the well using ropes and then dropped it. Then they closed all the shrines and locked them.

"Acharya, we could have hidden both boxes in that secret room. Why did you not want to do that?", asked Rangachari.

"It is not wise to keep all the wealth in one place.", said Pillai Lokacharyar.

Everyone sat in the *mandap* knowing that they were in great peril. Srinivasan and Thiruvengadam also reached there and joined them.

"Om Namo Narayanaya!", everyone chanted in unison. There was a loud rumble of thunder in the sky above.

In Thiruvengadam's house, Vellaayi held the casket with Namperumal inside it. She too heard the loud clap of thunder. It was followed by the sound of galloping horses. In a few moments, there were wails of "Narayana! Narayana!". A cold shiver ran through Vellaayi's spine.

5. The Hurricane

The rains hadn't come yet, but Srirangam already looked ravaged. The dark clouds in the heavy sky made day look like night. The winds seemed to make the trees dance like ghosts in the dark.. The dry leaves on the ground flew hither and thither as if they were seeking shelter. The cries of the birds sounded haunting. Inside Thiruvengadam's house, Vellaayi sat in the dark hugging the casket that had Namperumal in it. As her heart beat faster with every passing minute, it created vibrations on the wooden casket, which made her think that it was Namperumal's heart that was beating. As the rhythmic beat spread through her body, she fell asleep. She started dreaming. She stood in a dark dense forest, holding Namperumal in her hands - not the casket, but the shiny deity of Namperumal. She walked carefully, cradling Namperumal like a baby. The dark dense forest appeared more terrifying with the occasional lightning that struck. The strong winds from the hurricane showered dry leaves onto her, which felt like a thousand arrows simultaneously released from a bow. Somewhere in the distance, a wolf howled. Vellaayi trembled. She picked up pace as she walked through the forest. Soon, she was running. In the dark bushes to her side, numerous eyes appeared for a few seconds, and then disappeared. Before she could

understand what they were, a pack of wolves chased at her. She ran as fast as she could. She felt as if she was approaching the top of a hill. She just kept running - there was no time to think. She stopped only when she had reached the top of the hill. She looked down ahead and saw a ferocious ocean. The tides of the ocean rose very high as they hit the rocks on the side of the hill. It was all terrifying for Vellaayi. The wolves seemed to be nearing her with every passing second. She looked towards Namperumal in her hand, but was shocked to find that Namperumal was not in her hands anymore. She looked around in a state of despair, but couldn't see a thing in the darkness. She became teary-eyed. A bolt of lightning struck on the horizon, and a ball of light fell next to her. In the center of the light, Namperumal appeared in his living form. He looked at Vellaayi and smiled gently, calming her.

"Why have you stopped, Vellaayi? Come with me. Why do you fear the *Thiruparkadal*[21]?", he said to her.

Without waiting for her reply, he walked in the direction of the ocean and disappeared into thin air. Vellaayi looked at the ocean again. It now appeared to be calm like the heavenly ocean. The dark clouds dispersed, revealing the full moon. The moonlight was reflected on the calm waters of the ocean, making it look more beautiful.

---

[21] *Heavenly ocean surrounding Vishnu's abode in heaven.*

"Om Namo Narayanaya", she chanted and jumped into the ocean.

The sound of heavy thunder woke Vellaayi. She realized that she was sitting in Thiruvengadam's house. She heard the galloping of an army of horses. In moments, there were heart-wrenching cries of "Narayana! Narayana!". A cold shiver ran down Vellaayi's spine.

The inner area of the Srirangam temple looked like a battlefield. Malik Kafur was sitting in the *mandap* close to the east entrance of the temple. His soldiers stood along the walls of the temple. Pillai Lokacharyar was sitting in front of him with a worried look on his face. Rangachari, Srinivasan, Thiruvengadam and a few other priests of the temple stood beside him. They all appeared wounded - some had wounds on their faces, others on their hands or legs. They did not seem to care about the severe pain they were in. They held back their tears because they didn't want to appear vulnerable. It was evident that they had been tortured.

"Acharya, tell me where Namperumal is", said Malik Kafur.

"You did see inside the shrine as well, Namperumal is not here", said Pillai Lokacharyar confidently.

"This is not the answer I'm looking for! Until you tell me the location of Namperumal, I will torture them.", he said pointing towards the men who stood beside Pillai Lokachaarayar.

As he spoke, one of his soldiers punched Thiruvengadam's face hard. Thiruvengadam fell to the ground shouting "Narayana!".

He then kicked him.

"Narayana!"

"No!... Please stop this… Please stop this", shouted Pillai Lokacharyar.

"Then tell me where Namperumal is." Malik Kafur got up as he spoke these words. He took his sword from its sheath.

"If you don't, all of these men will fall to my sword!", he roared.

Heavy thunder rolled in the sky. But what Pillai Lokacharyar said next felt even heavier to Thiruvengadam, Rangachari, Srinivasan and the temple priests.

"I'll tell you… I'll tell you", he said as he closed his eyes, "Narayana! Please forgive me."

"No, don't! Our lives are insignificant compared to the Lord. Don't tell him anything just to save our worthless lives. We are all ready to sacrifice our lives for the Lord", pleaded Thiruvengadam.

"Yes! We are ready to sacrifice ourselves!", said Pillai Lokacharyar's disciples and the priests.

As soon as they said this, hard blows rained down on them. They all cried, "Narayana!"

"I said that I'll tell you where Namperumal is. Why are you still torturing them?", said Pillai Lokacharyar.

He then looked at Thiruvengadam and the priests.

"The Lord wouldn't condone sacrificing your lives - lives that were dedicated to his service. If I were to let that happen, there would be no bigger sinner than me", he said. Before anyone of them could respond, he looked at Malik Kafur.

"When our King Sundarapandian had got the news of your army plundering the temples, he had sent his men here two days ago to take Namperumal to Madurai.", he said.

"What? To Madurai?", asked Malik Kafur, shocked.

Rangachari, Srinivasan and the temple priests did not understand what was happening.

Malik Kafur thought for a while.

"How do I believe what you are saying? We will comb through every nook and corner of this town. If you're lying, and we find Namperumal somewhere here, I will kill all of you!", he said ferociously.

At that very moment, two of his soldiers came inside the temple. They brought a man along with them. It was boatman Kannan. He appeared shocked at what he saw there. Pillai Lokacharyar seemed expressionless.

"Captain, he is a boatman. He and a few boatman families have come to the temple along with their belongings. They say there will be floods in Kaveri very soon", said one of the soldiers.

"Is this true?", asked Malik Kafur, looking towards Kannan.

"Yes, it is true. There are dark clouds in the west. Strong winds are blowing. Even the astrologer had predicted very heavy rainfall this year. We were afraid that all our huts would be washed away in the flood. Hence, we have come to the temple for shelter until the storm subsides.", said Kannan breathlessly.

Malik Kafur sank into deep thought once again.

"If there are floods, the water level in the river could rise significantly. In that case, we wouldn't be able to take the horses by boat. We could end up being stuck here for a long time. These soldiers that had come to capture Warangal, and ended up coming much further south based on my promise of the wealth that we could loot here, might get restless and angry. They might even revolt. If that happens, my dream of capturing Madurai would be shattered. I would have to answer to emperor Alauddin. On the other hand, if we cross the river before the floods, we could reach Madurai easily. My other forces would also reach Madurai by then. But... But.. How can I leave Srirangam empty-handed? Is it true what they are saying about Namperumal? Who wouldn't try to save a statue made of *Abaranji* gold? I should find out soon if there is any truth in what they are saying.", he thought.

There was lightning on the horizon. Heavy thunder struck again. He looked at Pillai Lokacharyar.

"Even if I were to believe that Namperumal is not here right now, I have heard about the enormous amount of other treasures and wealth here. Give them to me, and I will leave this place. If I don't get those, then I'll slay all of you before I leave!", he raged.

"If you promise me that there will not be any deaths here, then I will show you what we have", said Pillai Lokacharyar.

"Hmm. I promise."

"A large wooden box filled with gold is inside that well". As Pillai Lokacharyar uttered these words, it started to rain.

Over the next hour, Malik Kafur's men got into the well and took out the wooden box. Malik Kafur was ecstatic on seeing the amount of gold in the box. He and his army took the box with them and crossed the Kaveri. The rains came down hard on Srirangam.

Like the wetness left behind by a heavy rain, which takes it's time to go away, the impact of Malik Kafur attack remained in Srirangam for many days. When a country is filled with prosperity and happiness, people are often involved in their work in a selfish way. But when the country is in trouble, selfishness tends to vanish, and people often display the best of humane qualities - love, helpfulness, kindness, and empathy. Likewise, the people of Srirangam came together to repair the damage left behind by Malik Kafur's army. They nursed the wounded. Everyone praised Pillai Lokacharyar's presence of mind. He did feel sad for having told a lie, but everyone consoled him by telling him that a lie uttered in order to save so many lives was well within *dharma*[22]. All told, Vellaayi was shaken. Her life had been a breeze until Malik Kafur came, and now it looked like it was caught in a hurricane. She tended to Thiruvengadam. She gave the wooden casket with Namperumal to Pillai Lokacharyar. The people of Srirangam conducted a festival for Namperumal. Seeing Namperumal in festive attire, Vellaayi felt overwhelmed. However, she also felt a strange uneasiness.

"These people put their lives on the line to save Namperumal. But I was sitting safe in some dark room. Namperumal had once appeared in my dream asking me to save him. I'd promised him that I would. But I have failed. All these people have gone through torture that I should have gone through. Oh, Lord! If ever such a thing happens again, I won't be sitting idle.", she thought deeply and promised herself.

She believed that the heartbeat she had felt in the wooden casket carrying Namperumal was now beating inside her. She felt that she had more rights over Namperumal than anyone else in Srirangam. In addition, Pillai Lokacharyar showed a great deal of kindness towards her post that incident. He had

---

[22] *Religious and moral law governing individual conduct (as per Hinduism).*

involved her in some of the temple duties. All these only increased Vellaayi's love for Namperumal. She decided to get married to Namperumal. Her mother Ponni was married to the Lord Arangan and did not enter into any other relationship with any man. This further encouraged Vellaayi in her thought process.

Although many historians have written about Malik Kafur's attempt to capture Madurai, a quick summary here will help maintain continuity of this story. It is good to start with how Malik Kafur had reached Thiruvellarai. After capturing Warangal, Malik Kafur and his army had marched further south to wage war against the Pandyas in order to capture Madurai. After the death of Maravarman Kulasekara Pandyan, his sons Veerapandya and Sundarapandya squabbled over which one of them would become the next king of Madurai. But when they came to know about Malik Kafur and his army marching towards their kingdom, Veerapandya left with an army to fight them, while Sundarpandya secured the fort of Madurai. In a place called Kannanur near Tiruchirapalli, a huge war broke out. Veerapandya's forces were defeated by Malik Kafur's army. When King Veerapandya was injured, his loyal guards took him into the Kollimalai forest. Malik Kafur's men wanted to capture and kill Veerapandya, but were unable to find him. In order to give themselves a better chance at capturing Veerapandya, Malik Kafur divided his large army into smaller groups and sent them towards Madurai on different routes. He led one group and arrived at Thiruvellarai. By the time they crossed Srirangam and reached Madurai, the other groups also joined them. With an army comprising many thousands of elephants, horses and foot soldiers he besieged the fort of Madurai. However, Sundarapandian had already made arrangements for the fort to be self-sufficient for many months by stocking up on food supplies and other basic needs. He had closed the iron gates of the fort. The moat around the fort prevented anyone from gaining access to the doors. Malik Kafur's men couldn't get into the fort even after trying for a month. Meanwhile, monsoon had set in, and the rains began. As their own food supplies started to dwindle, Malik Kafur's men were forced to return to Delhi. They looted much wealth on their way back, which they presented to Alauddin. The emperor was delighted, and gifted the men with many *maund*[23]*s* of gold.

Eleven years passed. On a July morning, Vellaayi was dancing in front of the temple of Arangan. A large crowd had gathered around the mandap to watch her perform. She had grown into a beautiful young woman of twenty-two. There was likely no woman in Srirangam who was not jealous of her beauty, nor a man who was not attracted to her. When she danced, the streets of Srirangam became quieter, the stoves were turned off, the birds in the trees stopped their chirping - even children couldn't be heard. All of Srirangam gathered around the stage where she danced. The only sound that echoed through the town was from her anklets. The expressions on her face, the

---

[23] *An Indian unit of weight equal to about 82 pounds (37 kg).*

mudra[24]s she displayed with her hands, and her perfectly choreographed steps were so beautiful that one felt that the dream of the great saint Bharatha - who invented the dance form of Bharatanatyam - had come alive. Those who watched her dance were mesmerized by its sheer beauty that they forgot about everything else including hunger or thirst.

Vellaayi's friend Rohini, a woman with a wheatish complexion and a frail body structure, was singing *pasurams* from the Naachiyar Thirumozhi written by Andal. Vellaayi danced to the tune and portrayed the words of the song through her dance.

Mannu perum puhazh madavan mamanivannan
mani mudi maindan

tannai uhandadu kaaranamaaha en sangu izhakkum
vazhakku unde

punnai kurukkatti naazhal serundi podumbinil
vaazhum kuyile

panni eppodum irundu viraindu en pavala vaayan
vara koovaai

Andal describes that as she was attracted to the Lord and always immersed in His thought, she had

---

[24] *A symbolic hand gesture typically used in Indian dance.*

grown so frail that her bracelet slipped down her hand and got lost. She asks the *koel* bird nested on the tree to ask the Lord on her behalf as to why He hadn't done anything about it. She asks the *koel* to sing in its sweet voice and tell the Lord to come by her side. Similar to how Andal was immersed in her love for the Lord, Vellaayi - dancing to the *pasuram* - was also filled with a great deal of love for Namperumal.

In those 11 years, a lot had changed in Vellaayi's life, as well as in the town of Srirangam. After Malik Kafur's siege, life in Srirangam was not the same. The schools that once taught the *Vedas*[25] and dance now taught the skills of self-defence and sword-fighting. Both women and men learned the art of war. Along with the sounds of the bell from the temple, the chanting of the *Vedas*, and singing of *pasurams*, now one could hear the sound of swords clashing as well. This was because everyone believed that Malik Kafur's raid was not the end, but just a beginning. As a cat would return to the kitchen after having tasted milk there, they believed that the taste of wealth in Srirangam would bring back the enemy again. They felt that they had a great responsibility to protect the Lord who had protected them for so long. They took turns standing guard around the temple every day. Vellaayi also learned self-defense and sword-fighting. Two years prior, her mother Ponni was affected by pneumonia and had passed away to her heavenly

---

[25] *The most ancient Hindu scriptures, written in early Sanskrit. The four chief collections of Vedas are the Rig Veda, Sama Veda, Yajur Veda, and Atharva Veda.*

abode. After this, Vellaayi felt very lonely. Thiruvengadam used to visit her often and provide some help. Vellaayi spent a lot of time performing her temple duties. She now believed that her life was completely dedicated to Namperumal. She felt that one day He would come and take her along with Him.

Once her dance was over, Vellaayi went home. But when she arrived there, a nasty surprise awaited her. A bullock cart was parked in front of her house. A horse was tied to the pole nearby. There were a couple of helpers standing with plates full of gifts. She walked up to them for a closer look. An apparently rich man, dressed in silk attire, with a neatly trimmed mustache, was seated on her verandah with great swagger. It was none other than Bhoopathi.

6. The Wedding

Escaping alive from the hands of Malik Kafur had made Bhoopathi the talk of the town. Sensing an opportunity to make a name for himself, he conveniently embellished the story of his encounter with Malik Kafur and his forces. He claimed that he had snatched a sword from one of the soldiers, engaged many of them in combat and forced them to flee. To make his story more believable, Bhoopathi now always carried a sword with him. He claimed that the army that had fled was the one that had looted Srirangam. He even boasted that if he were in Srirangam when they had attacked, they wouldn't have succeeded in taking away even a single stone from Srirangam. Many in Srirangam believed him. The rest didn't seem to care. In any case, Bhoopathi was now a more respected man in Srirangam, and because of this, he started frequenting Srirangam more often. His desire for Vellaayi grew by the day. He asked her to live with him on many occasions. After Ponni's death, he started harassing Vellaayi even more. Now, he was at her doorstep.

When Vellaayi reached her house, Bhoopathi spoke to her overbearingly.

"Vellaayi, come here. I've been waiting for you. Have you finished your song and dance at the temple?"

"What are you here for? Who are you to wait for me?", she shouted in disgust.

"It's not just me waiting for you. My love awaits you, my wealth awaits you! Ask for anything your heart desires - and I shall get it done for you. Why do you suffer in this hut? I'll build a palace for you. All you need to do is acknowledge my love for you."

"Keep your wealth to yourself! Now leave!". Vellaayi's anger rose.

"You want me to go now? Then tell me when you want me to come again."

"Don't ever come here again. Just get lost!"

Just then, Thiruvengadam arrived. He could sense what was going on.

"Bhoopathi, it would be a great help if you could just go away from here without creating any trouble", he said looking at Bhoopathi.

"Who are you to tell me where I should or should not go?", Bhoopathi raged.

"A man should not visit the house of a woman living alone", Thiruvengadam said.

"Then why are you here? Are you not a man?", Bhoopathi laughed sarcastically.

Thiruvengadam felt so utterly embarrassed that - for a moment - he wished he were dead.

"You needn't bother about whether he's a man or not. If you speak one more word against him, you will not go back alive!", Vellaayi shouted, eyes blood-red, as she drew a small knife from a sheath that hung around her waist. By this time, people had started gathering around them. Seeing the crowd, Bhoopathi started to walk away realizing that it was probably best to leave.

As he left, he looked at Vellaayi and said, "Girl, don't be angry for no reason. Devadasis have always needed the support and blessings of rich men. Don't forget that. I'll be back later." He then walked away and the crowd dispersed, leaving Vellaayi and Thiruvengadam alone.

This incident saddened Thiruvengadam and Vellaayi. "Devadasis have always needed the support and blessings of rich men. Don't forget that." - these words echoed in their heads. After a long silence, Thiruvengadam said - "Listen to me Kodhai, you are now of marriageable age. I don't know how much longer I'll be alive. I should get you married to a nice man as soon as possible. That's the only way to keep evil men like Bhoopathi away from you. I will go and meet the astrologer regarding finding a groom for you.", he said.

Vellaayi sat near Thiruvengadam and held his hand affectionately. He was still shaking from the shock of the incident. She consoled him. Then she said firmly - "Grandpa, I have decided to get married to Namperumal. I cannot marry anyone else."

Thiruvengadam tried hard to change her mind but to no avail. He then came to terms with it, thinking that this was probably the wish of the Lord himself.

"You are as stubborn as your mother. I can't win an argument with you. There is only one way now. You should get the *Deekshai* of Namperumal. This will make you belong to him. No other man would even think of coming near you.", he said.

"Then I should get the *Deekshai* as soon as possible!", she said enthusiastically.

"Oh Lord Namperumal! Bless this girl.", prayed Thiruvengadam.

Thiruvengadam started the process of getting Vellaayi married to Namperumal. He took her to Pillai Lokacharayar and told him about her wish to get married to Namperumal.

"Dear child, do you really understand how your life will be if you go ahead with your decision?" asked Pillai Lokacharayar, looking at Vellaayi.

"Acharya, I understand this very well. My mother had devoted her whole life to Lord Arangan. That way of life is not unknown to me. I already accepted Namperumal as my husband in my heart a few years ago. I am ready to lead my life according to the right way stipulated for one who is married to the Lord.", she said.

Pillai Lokacharayar closed his eyes and chanted, "Om Namo Narayana!"

The temple bell rang at that very moment. A gentle smile appeared on his face. He then opened his eyes and looked at Vellaayi.

"Namperumal has given his consent to the marriage. I must explain to you the rules of the life that you would have to lead once you are married to Namperumal. You should follow these five rules for the rest of your life.

1. You should pray to the Lord three times a day.

2. You should not consume meat.

3. You should observe fasts during auspicious festival days.

4. You should not have a relationship with any other man.

5. You should not entertain negative thoughts in your mind.

Do you agree to follow these rules for the rest of your life?"

"I might forget to breathe, but I will not forget to follow these rules", Vellaayi said confidently.

Pillai Lokacharyar smiled. Then he looked toward Thiruvengadam.

"Thiruvengadam, there is nothing more to contemplate. Have you chosen the symbol of God that would be used for the marriage?", he asked.

"Ah! Yes, I have brought it with me.", Thiruvengadam said as he pulled out something wrapped in a silk cloth from his bag. He removed the silk cloth. He held a white conch shell.

"You have chosen the most apt symbol for Vellaayi", said Pillai Lokacharyar with a broad smile, as he looked at the conch shell, "Keep this at the feet of the Lord for a month. Perform *pooja*[26] everyday. On the Wednesday that comes thirty days after today, let the marriage ceremony happen."

Vellaayi prostrated at the feet of Pillai Lokacharyar. He blessed her and left. Thiruvengadam was teary-eyed. He quickly wiped his tears using the towel on his shoulder. He and Vellaayi then walked towards their home.

For the wedding ceremony between a Devadasi and the Lord, a symbol of God was chosen as His manifestation. The girl would get 'married' to that symbol. For Vellaayis's wedding, Thiruvengadam

---

[26] *Act of worship.*

chose the white conch shell that Lord Vishnu held in his hand. Devadasis who did not enter into any relationship with any other man would receive an emblem of God imprinted on them by the priest of the temple. This process was referred to as *Devadasi Deekshai*. Pillai Lokacharyar explained the rules of this *Deekshai* to Vellaayi. When Bhoopathi heard about the wedding, he was angry. Even though he lusted for Vellaayi, he felt it was best to not do anything about it at the moment. He knew that if he took her away by force, the people of Srirangam would not let him get away with it. He decided to wait for the right time.

In the month that followed, Vellaayi's joy knew no bounds. She started to prepare for her wedding ceremony along with her dear friend Rohini. Rohini wove a beautiful blue silk saree for Vellaayi's wedding.

"What an apt color this is! It is akin to the blue-colored body of Lord Vishnu - He who safeguards the universe!", exclaimed Vellaayi joyfully as she held the saree in her hand. She hugged Rohini.

"Hmm... You see Lord Vishnu in everything. I suppose you don't see the rest of us." sighed Rohini.

"Half of what you say is true."

"Which half?"

"That I see Lord Vishnu all the time in all things I see is true. That I don't think about you is false."

"If you are always thinking about the Lord, how will you even have thoughts of us?"

"The Lord whom I think about every moment always thinks about all of us. Isn't thinking about him equivalent to thinking about all of you?", said Vellaayi naughtily.

"There's no use arguing with you!", Rohini said, and they both broke into laughter.

The big day finally arrived. Vellaayi and Rohini woke up before sunrise, went to the Kaveri and bathed. After they returned, Rohini ground sandalwood paste and applied it to Vellaayi's body. Vellaayi wore a white silk saree and went to the temple along with Rohini. Thiruvengadam was already waiting for them there. He was anxiously overseeing the arrangements for the ceremony. When he saw Vellaayi walking in, he froze for a moment. Even if a girl was being married to the Lord Himself, who can deny the unsaid sadness of a parent giving away their child? Thiruvengadam composed himself, and spoke.

"Kodhai, you go and get *Deekshai* first, then we can get started with the wedding ceremony.", he said as he patted her head gently. Vellaayi prostrated before him to seek his blessings. Both of them realized that this would be the last time that she would be seeking his blessings this way. She would not prostrate before anyone once she got married to Lord Namperumal. Thiruvengadam blessed her, as tears rolled down his cheeks. He then looked at Rohini.

"Can you take her to get *Deekshai*?", he said.

"I will take care of it, Grandpa. Don't you worry", said Rohini.

She took Vellaayi into the inner shrine, and made her sit in the *mandap* in front of the sanctum sanctorum. The priest of the shrine came towards them and asked Vellaayi "Are you ready to get *Deekshai*?"

"Yes, I'm ready.", said Vellaayi.

He then went back to take two iron rods that were dipped into a large cauldron of burning coal. One of the rods had the symbol of the conch shell on its tip while the other rod had the symbol of the *Sudarshana Chakra*[27]. Both of these symbols of Vishnu burned a bright hot red on the rods. Rohini carefully pulled Vellaayi's saree slightly down her left shoulder. The priest pressed both symbols onto the fair skin on Vellaayi's shoulder in one swift movement. Rohini couldn't bear the sight of it. She closed her eyes and turned away. Vellaayi was in a trance. In those few seconds, expressions of love, affection, and joy all danced on her face. Thiruvengadam stood near, holding back tears.

"Om Namo Narayana!", the crowd standing around the *mandap* chanted in unison. Rohini opened her eyes and turned towards Vellaayi. The mark of the

---

[27] *A spinning, disk-like weapon literally meaning "disk of auspicious vision," having 108 serrated edges used by Lord Vishnu.*

Tapta Mudra[28] comprising the symbols of a conch shell and *Sudarshana Chakra* had been deeply etched in Vellaayi's shoulder. She immediately took a peacock feather, dipped it in honey from a silver goblet, and ran the feather over the burn mark of the *Tapta Mudra* on Vellaayi's shoulder. Vellaayi was still in a trance, and gazed unblinkingly at Namperumal placed in the sanctum sanctorum.

After a while, the wedding ceremony began. The *mandap* was decorated with hangings of garlands made of flowers and coconut tree leaves. In the center of the *mandap*, the conch shell that Thiruvengadam had bought for Vellaayi's wedding ceremony was placed. The auspicious wedding thread known as the *mangal sutra*[29] was kept near it. It was made of gold. The priest showed the sacred flame of a lamp kept on a plate to Namperumal. He then brought it and showed it in front of the conch shell. Then he took 3 spoons of holy water from a small copper tumbler and sprinkled it on top of the shell.

"Bring the bride.", he said.

Vellaayi walked in along with her friends into the *mandap*. She wore the blue silk saree that Rohini had presented her. She had a beautiful red pendant on her forehead. Her hair was braided like Andal with jasmine flowers rolled over it. The silver anklets on her legs

---

[28] *A heated metal symbol (made of copper or gold) depicting a conch and the Sudarshana Chakra, that is stamped/applied on the body.*
[29] *A necklace that the groom ties around the bride's neck, in the Indian subcontinent.*

danced in unison announcing the arrival of the bride. She felt shy as she slowly walked into the *mandap*. Thiruvengadam was overwhelmed with joy. Vellaayi's friends sang the *pasuram* from Thirumozhi written by Aandal, that described the dream of her wedding with the Lord Vishnu.

Vaaranam aayiram soozha   valam vandhu ,

Naarana Nambi nadakkindraan yendredhir,

Poorana pokudam vaithu , puramengum ,

Thoranam naatta kana kanden thozhi , naan.

Indhiran ullitta devar kuzhaam yellam ,

Vandhirundhu yennai makal pesi mandhirithu,

Manthira kodi uduthi , mana maalai ,

Anthari chootta kanaa kanden thozhi naan

The visuals in front of Thiruvengadam's eyes suddenly changed. The decorations in the *mandap* disappeared. The crowd around the *mandap* disappeared. He only saw a 7-year-old Vellaayi dancing to the *pasuram*. Her dance conveyed the meaning of the *pasuram*. As the lines

"Maddalam kotta vari sangam nindru oodha ,

Muthudai thamam   nirai thaazhntha pandhar keezh,

Maithunan nambi madhu soodanan vandhu   yennai,

Kaithalam paththa kanaa kanden thozhi, naan."

were sung, the visuals changed again. In the *mandap* that was decorated with garlands, Vellaayi now stood as a beautiful grown woman, dressed as a bride. In place of the conch shell, Namperumal stood, dressed as a bridegroom. Vellaayi placed the garland in her hands around Namperumal's neck. He put the garland that he was holding around her neck. He then tied the *mangal sutra* around Vellaayi's neck, and then held both her hands tightly. As the *Getti Melam*[30] was played, Thiruvengadam came back to his senses. He saw that the garland that Vellaayi had held was now on the conch shell. The garland that was near the conch shell was now on Vellaayi's neck. The golden *mangal sutra* shone on her chest. He wiped his tears with the towel he had on his shoulder. He looked up to the sky. "Ponni, look at your daughter, she is a married woman now.", he said to himself. Pillai

---

[30] *Traditional wedding tune played on the 'nadaswaram' drums.*

Lokacharyar came and gave some holy water to Vellaayi to drink.

"Vellaayi, you have become *Nithya sumangali*[31] as you are now married to Namperumal", he said.

At that very moment there was some commotion outside the *mandap*. Soon, the crowd made way for a man to come towards the *mandap*. He was in his fifties, but his face had the glow of a much younger man. Two of his disciples stood behind him. Pillai Lokacharyar's face brightened as he recognized the man.

"Venkatanatha! Is that you? This is such an auspicious day!", Pillai Lokacharyar said as he walked towards the visitor. It was in fact none other than Vedanta Desikar - who was considered God's own child.

Vedanta Desikar was the disciple of Appular who was a direct disciple of the great saint Ramanujar. He was a man of great wisdom, also a Vaishnavaite. Before he was born, his parents had gone to the holy temple of Thirupathi to seek blessings from the Lord for a child. That night as the couple were sleeping, Lord Vishnu appeared in the dream of Desikar's mother in the form of a Vaishnavite child. He made her swallow the small bell that was kept in the sanctum sanctorum. The next morning, the priest who had gone to perform the pooja rituals was shocked to find

---

[31]*Female who is married to the Lord and thus would never be a widow.*

the bell missing. As everyone started looking for it frantically, the Lord spoke in the form of an Oracle.

"Don't search for the bell. I have given it to a mother who is now carrying a child who will grow into a wise saint - just like Ramanujar."

The couple named the son born to them Venkatanathan. The child impressed everyone with his wisdom. He was popularly addressed as Vedanta Desikar. As he grew up, he served at the temple of Kanchipuram Varadharaja Perumal temple and wrote numerous poems on the Lord.

Now his arrival surprised Pillai Lokacharyar.

"Any day that I get to visit the Lord's abode in Srirangam is an auspicious day for me.", said Vedanta Desikar with a gentle smile.

But soon, his face turned grim.

"What happened, Venkatanatha? Is something troubling you?", asked Pillai Lokacharyar.

"Yes Acharya, grave danger is coming to Srirangam. I'm here to warn you.", he said in a hushed tone. But Vellaayi, standing behind Pillai Lokacharyar, heard his words clearly. A wave of uneasiness ran through her body. Visions from eleven years ago flashed before her eyes.

Pillai Lokacharyar hesitated for a moment as he looked around. Then he looked at Desikar.

"Come with me. Let's speak in private.", he said.

He took Desikar and his disciples to the *mutt*[32] situated behind the temple. The crowd dispersed from the temple.

That night, Vellaayi was at her home alone. Next to her was the conch shell that was used as a manifestation of the Lord during the wedding ceremony. Her subconscious mind seemed to be warning her about the impending danger to Srirangam. After a long time contemplating this, she fell asleep, and dreamt.

On a full moon night, Vellaayi ran towards the inner shrine of the temple. The temple premises resembled a war zone. She ran towards the inner shrine, but crashed into a wall and fell back. In the dim moonlight that pierced through the holes in the roof of the temple, she could see parts of the wall before her. Confused, she wondered how a new wall got there. She started to walk along the wall, keeping her hands against it for guidance. She seemed to be walking around in a maze, and lost her sense of direction. A ray of light appeared at a distance, and she ran towards it. And then she was shocked - as she found herself right where she started - at the entrance to the inner shrine. She went inside again, walked along the twists and turns again, and again ended up where she started.

"Where is Arangan? Where is Namperumal?", she thought as tears rolled down her cheeks. Her eyes fell upon the east temple tower. Something made her run

---

[32] *Sanskrit word that means institute or college or monastery.*

towards it. She ran up the stairs of the tower to get to the top floor. There was Namperumal - sitting near a wall! She ran towards him and fell at his feet.

"Oh, Lord! What happened? Why are you here?", she asked, stuttering.

"Kodhai, it is time for me to stay away from Srirangam for a while.", he said.

"What are you saying? What will I do without you? What sort of calamity has befallen us that has made you take this decision?", she asked breathlessly.

"Bad times lay ahead of us for the next few years. Many a peril will be averted if I stay away."

"How can the Lord himself have bad times?"

"There are rules that apply in this world. Even the Lord is subject to those rules when living in this world.", Namperumal said.

"Will the calamity be averted by you going away?"

"It cannot be entirely averted. However, we could reduce the damage it could cause - and try to safeguard the future as best we can. For that to happen, I should stay away from Srirangam for a while."

"Please take me along with you my Lord!", she pleaded.

"Very soon, the time will come when I will take you along with me. But for now, Srirangam needs you.", he said.

A ball of light appeared in front of her eyes and disappeared - and Namperumal disappeared with it. She stood at a window on the top floor looking into the distance towards where the Lord seemed to have gone. In the warm moonlight, Srirangam looked serene and peaceful below. However, Vellaayi felt no calm within, as waves of sadness and fear engulfed her.

7. Danger

"A great deluge is imminent.", said Vedanta Desikar, as Pillai Lokacharyar listened wide-eyed.

"What are you saying, Venkatanatha? You had spoken about some danger earlier, but now you talk about a deluge?", he asked.

They were seated inside the *mutt* of Pillai Lokacharyar . Vedanta Desikar's disciples sat beside him. Pillai Lokacharyar's disciples Srinivasan and Rangachari were seated beside Pillai Lokacharyar. Their faces were grim.

"Yes Acharya. It's better that Vikraman here, disguised as my disciple, explains it.", he said looking at the man seated to his right.

"Disguised? You mean Vikraman is not actually your disciple?", asked Pillai Lokacharyar.

"No. Vikraman is a spy. You know how our temples were plundered by Malik Kafur. To be prepared for such attacks in the future, the Kanchipuram *Mutt* had employed some spies. These spies were deployed in the north so that they could look out for signs of any threat to us, and keep us in the know. Vikraman is one of them. After hearing the news he brought yesterday, I had to bring him here to meet you", said Vedanta Desikar.

"What? Is there another attack being planned? Is Malik Kafur's army returning to attack us again?", asked Srinivasan, sounding concerned.

Vikraman who was silent until then, started to speak.

"No. A demon even crueler than him.", he said.

"Vikrama, let's not talk in metaphors anymore. Please be specific.", said Vedanta Desikar.

Vikraman stood up and started to walk. He stopped at a large window. It had been about 2 hours since the moon had risen in the night sky. He looked into the distance and started speaking as if he were describing a scene he was seeing.

"We all know how much Malik Kafur had looted from us here. However, he was still disappointed that he couldn't get his hands on the golden statue of Namperumal. He wanted to return with his forces to capture it. But his plans did not materialize due to power struggles within the kingdom. Emperor Alauddin Khalji had greatly trusted Malik Kafur and promoted him to higher ranks in the ministry. In three years, emperor Alauddin's health deteriorated. Malik Kafur stayed by his side and took care of him. As the days passed, he started to fancy his chances to take over the throne. He imprisoned and killed those who didn't favor him. He even imprisoned two of Alauddin's sons, and crowned the third son Shihabuddin - a child - as the prince. Alauddin became a mere puppet in Kafur's hands. In just a few days after

Shihabuddin's coronation as prince, Alauddin breathed his last. Malik Kafur now made Shihabuddin the emperor of Delhi and ruled the kingdom on his behalf. Some of Alauddin's men, who were incensed by all of this, plotted against Kafur, and successfully killed him one night while he was asleep in his room. After that, competition for Delhi's throne intensified. In the four years that followed, much blood was shed for the throne. Ultimately, two years ago, one of Alauddin's ministers named Ghaji Malik, who ruled the kingdom of Dibalpur put an end to all the gory killings and ascended the throne. He now rules Delhi in the name of Ghiyath al-Din Tughluq", said Vikraman. He then turned around and looked at the people sitting in the room.

"Now that Malik Kafur is no more, where is the danger to us?", asked Rangachari.

"He is dead, but his accounts of the riches in the South are very much alive. In particular, there are several stories of Namperumal doing the rounds among the Delhi forces. After Alauddin died, the King of Warangal, Prataparudra, had stopped paying taxes to Delhi. A year ago, Ulugh Khan, the son of Ghiyath al-Din Tughluq marched with an army to Warangal. However, his army could not penetrate the strong defense of Warangal. Upset with this, he executed many of his men who led the attack. He returned to Devagiri and came back with another army. This was a different kind of army - one that was made up of hardened criminals. They captured many a kingdom on their way to Warangal, looting wealth and killing anyone in their way. This time, when they reached Warangal, they employed an entirely different strategy, and successfully captured the fort. The city of Warangal now is practically a graveyard.", said Vikraman in a deeply troubled voice.

"What happened to King Pratapa Rudra?", asked Srinivasan.

"They were taking him to Delhi, but he died on the way."

"Narayana!", exclaimed both Srinivasan and Rangachari in unison.

"Warangal, which was essentially a protective fort for the whole of South India, has fallen. The army of looters could be here anytime soon.", said Vikraman.

"We should immediately inform our King in Madurai!", said Rangachari.

"We've taken care of that. A messenger has been sent to the King to inform him about this impending danger.", said Vedanta Desikar who had not spoken for a while. He then turned to Pillai Lokacharyar and said, "You might already know this, but internal squabbles are rife in the Pandyan Kingdom. Sundarapandian had sought the support of Pratapa Rudra to fight against his brother Veerapandiyan. Now that Pratapa Rudra is no more, I'm not sure how much help we will get from either of the Pandyas."

"I understand. You are suggesting that we make our own plans to face this threat.", said Pillai Lokacharyar.

"Yes we have to take matters into our own hands.", said Vedanta Desikar.

"Om Namo Narayana!", Pillai Lokacharyar chanted, closing his eyes. He then looked at Vedanta Desikar and asked, "Venkatanatha! What sort of arrangements do you have in mind?"

"Acharya, we should protect two things. First, the temple of Srirangam and the procession deities. Secondly, we should protect the women and children of Srirangam."

"You're right. Last time, thanks to the Lord's blessings, we were saved by the heavy rains. It would be foolish to think we might be as lucky this time."

"Yes Acharya. This time we should take the Namperumal statue to a much safer place. We should create a maze inside the main shrine such that the sanctum sanctorum is closed."

As Vedanta Desikar said those words, everyone in the room gasped in shock.

"What are you saying, Venkatanatha? Close down the sanctum sanctorum? That means we wouldn't be able to perform the prayers and rituals.", asked Pillai Lokacharyar.

"Yes Acharya, that is right. The situation at hand is grave. When there is a demise of someone associated with the temple, we have the practice of closing the temple. Similarly, on account of this extraordinary situation, stopping the prayers and rituals would not be wrong. We are the target of an army of looters. They will wreak havoc when they arrive. They are already leaving a trail of destruction on their way here. The best thing that we can do, is to raise a wall to protect the sanctum sanctorum", said Vedanta Desikar.

"Oh Lord! Why is this happening?", exclaimed Rangachari.

"If the desire of the Lord is so, then it will happen. You mentioned creating a maze inside the temple. For that we would need someone who is skilled in constructing such a maze.", said Pillai Lokacharyar.

Vedanta Desikar smiled. He looked at his second disciple who quietly sat near him.

"This person here, disguised as my second disciple Paramanandam, is skilled at construction. He will be able to construct the maze.", said Vedanta Desikar

Paramanandam bowed before everyone, nodding his head in agreement to whatever Desikar had said.

"You seem to have thoroughly thought this through, and have come with whatever we need to get started! Then you must have also thought about how to protect the women and children of Srirangam. Tell us your plan.", said Pillai Lokacharyar.

"When Malik Kafur had come, I heard you had hidden the women and children safely in some of the houses nearby. You also had to make those arrangements in the little time you had. But this time we have to be far more careful. Their army could very well break into houses. So I think we should send the women and children to other towns near Madurai.", he said.

"Hmm. That will be challenging - but it seems like we have little choice.", said Pillai Lokacharyar.

"When do you think they might attack?", asked Srinivasan.

"They have reached Mysore. They could be here in a month or two", said Vikraman.

"They could even be defeated on the way, correct?", asked Rangachari.

"Yes, that is a possibility - but we can't count on it. The lack of strong leadership in our kingdom could tilt the scales in our enemy's favour.", said Vikraman.

Silence filled the room for a while, until Pillai Lokacharyar broke it.

"The deluge approaching Srirangam is unprecedented. It is our duty to be prepared. Our preparation will affect temple operations, and so we should inform the newly appointed sthanikar Narasimha Moorthy accordingly. Then we should inform the people of Srirangam.", he said.

"Let's do it then.", said Vedanta Desikar.

The next day, Rangachari bought Narasimha Moorthy to the *mutt*. Narasimha Moorthy was the head administrator of the Srirangam temple. People like him who led the administration of temples were called *'sthanikars'*. They were appointed by the government.

Narasimha Moorthy was clad in a silk shirt and a silk dhoti. He wore a naamam on his forehead. He was about 6 feet tall. He keenly listened to the arrangements proposed by Vedanta Desikar.

Then he said, "Desikar, the plan you propose definitely makes sense. However, I believe we are panicking unnecessarily. During the invasion of Malik Kafur, there was lack of administration in the temple, hence Lokacharyar had to take matters into his own hands to protect the temple. Now the situation is different. We have soldiers who are appointed by the government. You said you have already sent the message to the King. Let us wait for orders from the King before proceeding with anything. We shouldn't be doing anything on our own.".

"The royals are distracted by infighting. If we wait for their orders, we may not be able to act in time.", said Vikraman.

"Without the King's orders, we cannot suspend temple activities.", said Narasimha Moorthy.

Before Vikraman could respond, Vedanta Desikar spoke.

"*Sthanikar*! I do understand your situation. But we might lose valuable time if we wait for orders from the King. You could go ahead and communicate our arrangements to the King. For now, the activities of the temple could continue as usual. However, let Paramanandam create a maze with secret pathways to the sanctum sanctorum within the temple. Once we receive the orders from the King, we shall close the existing pathways to the sanctum sanctorum. Does that sound better?"

After contemplating this for a few minutes, "Hmm.. as long as the activities in the temple are not hindered, it should be fine.", said Narasimha Moorthy.

"Good, now let us inform the people about these arrangements as well.", said Vedanta Desikar.

Everyone agreed.

In the *mandap* close to the east entrance of the temple, Pillai Lokacharyar was seated. Vedanta Desikar sat beside him. Rangachari, Srinivasan, Narasimha Moorthy, Vikraman and Paramanandam stood behind them. The priests of the temple stood facing them. Thiruvengadam also stood among them. Behind them were the people of Srirangam. Vellaayi and her friend Rohini stood at the front of the crowd. Boatsman Kannan stood behind them. Everyone seemed to be in shock. They couldn't stomach what

Vedanta Desikar just told them. It felt like wounds of the past were being reopened.

Namperumal's words from Vellaayi's dream echoed within her - "Srirangam needs your help now."

"What? Leaving Namperumal and going into hiding somewhere is so wrong. I have sworn to Namperumal that I would protect Srirangam. I can not run away in the face of danger.", thought Vellaayi.

"Acharya! Srirangam is also mine, and it is my duty to protect it. I would rather die protecting Srirangam than try to protect myself.", she said.

Every word she uttered pierced the silence of the crowd. As she finished speaking, the crowd erupted in unison - "Srirangam is also mine, I will never leave!"

Vedanta Desikar looked keenly at Vellaayi. He was surprised. Noticing this, Pillai Lokacharyar said, "The people of Srirangam consider Lord Arangan a member of their family. It is very difficult to separate them from their Lord."

"Hmm, I understand Acharya", said Vedanta Desikar. Closing his eyes, he chanted, "Om Namo Narayana!".

He then opened his eyes and looked towards the crowd.

"I am speechless in front of your selfless devotion towards the Lord. However, it is imperative we plan ahead to protect Srirangam. Paramanandam who has come with me is very skillful in building things. He would need your help in creating underground rooms in some of the houses in Srirangam. It could prove invaluable in times of danger. I hope you will cooperate with him on this.", he said.

"We will surely do it.", they said in unison.

Chants of "Om Namo Narayana!" from the crowd echoed through the streets of Srirangam and dissolved into the Kaveri.

Over the following month, work moved quickly. A maze was created inside the temple leaving gaps to reach the sanctum sanctorum. Vellaayi felt as though scenes from her dream were coming to life. Underground rooms were built in some of the houses in the town. The houses of Thiruvengadam and Srinivasan also had underground rooms built. All in all, preparations for 'wartime' were truly underway.

There was no response to the request Narasimha Moorthy had sent to the King. The day of *Kaisiga Ekadesi* arrived. Namperumal was taken to the banks of the Kaveri river, and after the rituals were performed, He was brought back to the *mandap* inside the temple. There is mention of *Kaisiga Ekadesi* in the Varaha Purana. In a small town called Thirukurungudi near Tirunelveli, the Lord Vishnu deity in the temple is known as Vainava Nambi. As the legend goes, many years ago, there was a man named Paanan Nampaaduvaan who had a great devotion towards

Vainava Nambi. He had kept a fast during the *Ekadesi*[33] in the month of Karthigai (November) and sang the *Kaisiga* hymn. On his way back home, he came face-to-face with a *Brahma Raakshas* (demon) who was waiting to eat him. However, he 'transferred' all the grace he had obtained from the Lord (from singing the *Kaisiga Pann*[34]) to the demon and thus released him from his curse. *Kaisiga Ekadesi* is the *Ekadesi* day that occurs thirty days before the *Vaikunta Ekadesi*[35] day. This was the festivity that was happening in Srirangam.

Vellaayi was dancing in front of Namperumal placed in the *mandap*. Thiruvengadam was singing the Thirupallaandu *pasuram* written by Periyazhwar. The song, constructed as a mother's words to her child, wishing her all sorts of goodness and happiness, was apt for the situation. This reflected the motherly love the people of Srirangam had for Lord Arangan.

Pallaandu pallaandu pallaayiraththaandu

---

[33] *A Sanskrit word for number 11, indicating the 11th day of each half of the month in the Vedic lunar calendar. It is considered a day to cleanse the body, aid repair and rejuvenation and is usually observed by partial or complete fast.*

[34] *Pann – a melodic mode used by the Tamil people in their music since ancient times.*

[35] *A special Ekadasi dedicated to Vishnu. It occurs in the Hindu calendar, in the month of Margashirsha (between December and January). When observed, it bestows liberation from the cycle of birth and death.*

pala kodi nooraayiram

mallaanda thin thol manivannaa! un

sevadi sevvi thirukkaappu

adiyomodum ninnodum pirivinri aayiram pallaandu

vadivaay nin vala maarbinil vaazhginra mangaiyum
pallaandu

vadivaarsodhi valaththuraiyum sudaraazhiyum
pallaandu

padaipor pukku muzhangum appaanjasanniyamum
pallaande

While everyone was mesmerized by Vellaayi's dancing, a man ran towards them from the banks of the Kollidam. He seemed frightened and said something anxiously to Vikraman. Vikraman went towards Vedanta Desikar, Pillai Lokacharyar and Narasimha Moorthy.

"The forces of Ulugh Khan have won the battle at Kannanur fort. No one can stop them from reaching Srirangam now.", he said.

"We should immediately put our safety measures in place.", said Vedanta Desikar.

"*Mangala Aarti*[36] would be done in about an hour. We can start the safety measures after that.", said Narasimha Moorthy.

There was some confusion about whether the *Mangala Aarti* was to be stopped immediately or if this opportunity of performing the *aarti* to their Lord 'one last time' was to be utilized. After a quick discussion they decided to complete the *Arathi* quickly. The ritual ended in the next hour.

Everyone chanted "Om Namo Narayana!"

Just then another man ran towards them. He looked at Vikraman and Vedanta Desikar.

"The evil force has reached the northern bank of the Kollidam. They might be here sooner than we thought.", he said, trembling.

Everyone was shocked to hear this. They never expected this to happen so soon. From the northern bank of the Kollidam, a big force was marching towards Srirangam. A battalion of horses, elephants and foot soldiers marched through the river causing gigantic ripples. In the middle was Ulugh Khan, as fierce as a Brahma Raakshas, leading them towards Srirangam. The deluge was near.

---

[36] *Daily predawn woorship ceremony honouring the Deity of the Supreme Lord, which brings auspiciousness (mangala) to the performer.*

8. The Deluge

When one has advance notice of a looming catastrophe, one might tend to overthink the options available to face it, and actually end up overlooking the best solution. By the same token, when calamity strikes without warning, one might just act quickly and end up taking the best way forward. The people of Srirangam found themselves in the latter situation. They hadn't expected Ulugh Khan's forces to reach the northern bank of Kollidam that quickly. All the arrangements that had been made had to be reviewed and redone as necessary. Paramanandam had completed work on underground secret rooms in ten houses in Srirangam. Thankfully, the necessary arrangements in those rooms to keep the old, women and children safe were in place. People proceeded to the respective rooms that they had been assigned to. Emotions were high, but everyone was trying to do what was told of them. Pillai Lokacharyar could see tears in the eyes of some as they moved about. Vedanta Desikar, Vikraman and Thiruvengadam approached him.

"Acharya! We had earlier decided that you would carry Namperumal to Madurai. But if you leave now, you'll probably be captured easily - as our enemies might already be in Uraiyur by the time you get there. We think it's better that you stay in the underground room in Thiruvengadam's house for now - and leave here when the time is right.", said Desikar.

"How can I hide, leaving all of you here to face the enemy?". Before he could even complete his question, Vedanta Desikar interrupted -

"Safeguarding Namperumal is your sacred responsibility. You have to lay low for a while.", he said.

Everyone hurried on with the arrangements as there was no time to lose. Rangachari got a wooden casket. They kept Namperumal in it and locked it. Thiruvengadam took the wooden casket and left for his house along with Pillai Lokacharyar. Vellaayi also joined them.

The underground room constructed in Thiruvengadam's house was spacious. Paramanadam had constructed it like a miniature hall. Many pillars supported the roof of the room. The room was stocked with food. Fruits and vegetables that wouldn't get spoilt easily were also stocked. The women, children, and the elderly who had already assembled in the room bowed before Pillai Lokacharyar. The lack of the usual cheer and enthusiasm on their faces when they sought his blessings didn't escape him. They seemed to be in shock. They placed the wooden casket with Namperumal on a seat at the corner of the room. Pillai Lokacharyar sat beside the casket. As he closed his eyes, tears rolled down his cheeks.

"Om Namo Narayana", he chanted.

Vellaayi, who was looking at him all this while, also got teary-eyed.

Meanwhile at the temple, Vedanta Desikar and Rangachari kept Ranganayaki's statue inside the underground storage that was set up behind the shrine.

"Acharya, couldn't we have kept Namperumal also in here?", asked Rangachari.

"The approaching forces are capable of utterly ransacking this place and even demolish the temple if they don't get Namperumal.", said Vedanta Desikar.

Rangachari did not have to say anything more. The fear in his eyes spoke volumes.

"Rangachari, we should visit Shrutha Prakashikacharya. We should protect him and the commentary he has written on Sri Ramanuja's *Sri Bhashyam*", said Vedanta Desikar.

Rangachari nodded, indicating that this was something important. Both of them walked through the East Chithirai street to reach the house of Sri Sudharsana Suri, who was also called Shruthaprakaiskachaarya. Sri Ramanuja has written a commentary on the *Vedanta Sutra*[37] written by Sri

---

[37] *The Vedanta Sutras (also called the Brahma Sutras) were written by the sage Vyasa (Bhadranarayana) to systematise the teachings of the Upanishads. Upanishads are philosophical texts delineating some of the key concepts within Hinduism, including notions of the soul, reincarnation, karma, and liberation.*

Bhadranarayana in his book *Sri Bhashyam*. Sri Sudarsana Suri had written his commentary on the *Sri Bhasyam* in his work *Shrutha Prakashika*. This rare literature explained the *Brahma Sutra*[38] for the common man. Hence, such a work was considered a treasure. In order to protect this, Vedanta Desikar and Rangachari had come to the house of Sudharsana Suri. There was an oil lamp lit inside the house. An old man sat beside it. His eyes were closed and his lips chanted the name of Lord Narayana. His two sons sat beside him. Vedanta Desikar went inside, bowed before him and sat on a seat in front of him.

"Acharya! Srirangam is in danger. I have come to take you and your work *Shrutha Prakashika* to a safe place. Please come with me now. We can leave Srirangam at an opportune time later.", he said.

Sri Sudarsana Suri opened his eyes and looked at Vedanta Desikar with warm affection.

"Venkatanaatha, it is very important to protect the *Shrutha Prakashika*. Generations to come will greatly benefit from it. The Lord has written it himself through me. I am just His instrument. I highly appreciate you having taken up this task. Please take the *Shrutha Prakashika*. But I will not come from here. What greater blessing could I have than to die where Lord Arangan is?", he asked.

---

[38] *Another name for Vedanta Sutras.*

"Acharya! How could we leave you behind?", said Vedanta Desikar, shocked.

"Where will you take this old man? I consider leaving this world from here, the place that is so close to Lord Arangan's heart, my greatest blessing". As Sri Sudarsana Suri spoke these words, he hesitated a little, and looked at his sons seated beside him. "My two sons are here. Please make them your disciples and take them along with you. Lord Arangan will take care of me", he said and closed his eyes again.

Vedanta Desikar sat in disbelief for a few moments. Rangachari gave him a nudge, and he came back to his senses. He took the *Shrutha Prakashika* and left along with the sons of Sudharsana Suri. All of them reached the East entrance of the temple and went inside. As they walked in, Vikraman closed the door shut behind them.

"Vikraman, have all the arrangements been done?", asked Vedanta Desikar.

"Yes everything is done. We just need to put stoppers to hold the gates tight", said Vikraman.

As they were talking, some commotion could be heard near the *mandap*, and they turned to look toward it. A small excited crowd had formed there. In the middle of the crowd stood Bhoopathi, sword in hand. His admirers were expectantly recounting stories of how he had supposedly 'defeated' Malik Kafur and his forces. They cheered for him thinking he would fight on their behalf. Bhoopathi was in fact too scared to speak. He was sweating, and his hands trembling, but he was trying to appear stoic. Rangachari felt disgusted seeing this. However, Vikraman took him away from there as there was work to be done. They closed all the four entrances to the temple and protected the gates with big stoppers.

"Nobody can easily break these and enter the temple. The soldiers responsible for protecting the temple are hiding on the walls and on the temple *gopurams*. They can use their arrows to take down anyone who tries to scale the wall.", said Vikraman.

"That's great, Vikraman. I think we've done the best that we could at this point. We must defend our temple and hold out against the attackers for as many days as possible. In the meantime, we will hopefully get some help from Madurai", said Vedanta Desikar.

Narasimha Moorthy, who stood beside Desikar, nodded in agreement.

When Ulugh Khan's forces crossed the Kollidam river and reached the northern entrance of the temple, the entire town looked deserted. However, the light emanating from the firewood torches within the temple premises lit up the sky. The smoke from the torches made the air warmer. As he saw the closed gates of the temple, Ulugh Khan's eyes reddened in anger, and this seemed to further raise the temperature of the moment. He looked around for an opening to enter the temple, and couldn't find any. He

had some of his men take a closer look. They went around, and came back disappointed.

"Alright, let's not wait anymore. Use our elephants to break the gates. Let some of our soldiers scale the wall of the temple and open the gates from the inside. Kill anyone who tries to stop you. I want Namperumal!", he growled.

Over the next few minutes, his soldiers used their elephants to uproot big trees, which they used to charge at the temple gates, but to no avail. Some of the soldiers went to the wall and proceeded to form a human ladder with each man climbing on to the shoulders of the next. They tried to scale the wall and jump inside the temple. Right away, a shower of arrows rained on them from both sides, collapsing the ladder formation. More soldiers tried to form the ladder again, but they faced the same fate. Ulugh Khan was furious. He ordered his men on the ground to shoot arrows at the soldiers hidden inside the temple *gopurams*. But this was easier said than done, as those soldiers were hiding behind the gopurams. When Ulugh Khan's men did shoot arrows, they ended up hitting and killing many of their own men who were trying to scale the wall. Chants of "Om Namo Narayana!" from inside the temple echoed like thunder in the sky. Ulugh Khan's anger grew. He called for one of his commanders named Khuroos Khan. Khuroos Khan was Ulugh Khan's favorite servant because he always carried out his orders unquestioningly.

"We can't wait any more, we should throw flames into the temple and burn it down. This temple must be under my control in the next hour!", he roared, sending shivers into some of his soldiers.

"So it be, my chief", said Khuroos Khan.

Once Khuroos Khan went ahead, a few other commanders came towards Ulugh Khan.

"Chief, please excuse us. We have already reduced so many temples to ashes. Can we ever wash away those sins? Many of our soldiers have since been lost to an unknown disease. We have heard that this is a very holy place. Let's not burn this one down. Let us leave. Instead, let's capture Madurai and become rulers of the kingdom. The wealth of this temple would then automatically become ours", said one of the commanders.

Ulugh Khan listened keenly. He looked at the commanders. He instantly calmed down, as if he had realized something. He smiled gently.

"You have given me great advice at the right time", he said as he dismounted his horse. He walked towards the commanders warmly as if to embrace them. They were relieved. Khuroos Khan was looking on carefully. As Ulugh Khan neared them, he pulled out his sword and beheaded all of them before anyone could react.

"I was born to rule the world. Are you asking me to run away being unable to break the protection of this small temple? Does anyone else have thoughts of leaving this place without capturing it?", he thundered. No one dared answer. Khuroos Khan smiled. He then looked at his forces in front of him and waved his hand. Each one of them took out what looked like a bamboo pipe from pouches tied around their waists, and held it in their hands. They filled it with some balls, and awaited further orders from Khuroos Khan.

Those inside the temple were unaware of what was happening outside. The silence felt like the lull before a storm. Suddenly, fireballs were raining down on them, causing explosions as they fell inside the temple. People were crying out in pain and falling to the ground. Those that were hit by the flames were burned instantly. It felt as though a large meteor had burst in the sky and broke into a million pieces, showering down fire upon them. In moments, the northern gate of the temple was in pieces. Smoke covered the entrance. Ulugh Khan emerged through the smoke. He looked carefully around the temple. His booming laughter then filled the air.

9. Gajendran's liberation

While the Sultanate[39] forces attacked kingdoms in the south of India, they were also fighting the Mongolian army in the north. They acquired the skill of using bombs from fighting the Mongolians, and this is what they had now used in Srirangam. Those inside the temple did not see this coming. They were shell-shocked, and were desperately trying to come to terms with what had just happened. They shuddered as they saw Ulugh Khan emerge from the smoke. Narasimha Moorthy who was standing in front, mustered the courage to approach Ulugh Khan. He stood before him, shivering. The others were now more shocked that Narasimha Moorthy had actually walked up to Ulugh Khan. Ulugh Khan looked carefully at Narasimha Moorthy, his eyes blood-red in anger.

"Sir, these are peace-loving people. They love Lord Arangan more than anything else. They love this temple more than they do their own lives. Please do not cause more damage to this temple. Please calm down.", said Narasimha Moorthy.

Ulugh Khan laughed so loud that it drowned out all other sounds there. The reflection of Narasimha Moorthy's shaking face could be seen in his eyes. In a

---

[39] *Governed or led by a Sultan (Muslim ruler).*

flash, he slashed his sword across Narasimha Moorthy's neck, beheading him. Blood splashed onto Ulugh Khan's face. Everyone froze in terror.

"If you do not want any more loss of life, hand over all the temple riches and Namperumal to me. I will spare your lives", Ulugh Khan roared.

But as he uttered these words, an arrow sped towards him. He instinctively moved out of its way just in time, and it hit the ground. He swiftly pulled out a dagger from his waist and threw it towards where the arrow had come from. It pierced the heart of the soldier on the wall of the temple. As the soldier thudded to the ground, Ulugh Khan's men advanced. The other soldiers in the temple advanced towards the forces of Ulugh Khan. Seeing this, the people of Srirangam who were in the temple also advanced. In moments, war broke out. Both sides battled fiercely. The people of Srirangam weren't trained to fight, but the energy and intent they showed surprised the Sultanate forces. Vikraman stood protecting Vedanta Desikar. Bhoopathi's followers were emboldened by his presence and advanced. Bhoopathi had to move ahead, but fear wore heavy on his feet. As he fell behind his followers, they in turn fell prey to Ulugh Khan's sword.

As Bhoopathi stood paralyzed, an enemy soldier ran towards him. The soldier suddenly went flying back many feet away as if thunder had struck him. Rangachari stood there with a heavy wooden club in his hands. His gaze briefly met Bhoopathi's. The contempt in Rangachari's eyes could have reduced Bhoopathi to ashes, but Rangachari quickly shifted his focus to two other enemy soldiers. Rangachari ran towards them like a raging bull. Bhoopathi slipped away towards the temple entrance and started running towards the bank of the Kaveri. Meanwhile, Rangachari took down two more enemies. The club in his hand looked like Bheema's *Gadha* (mace). But his end was nearing. A spear hit him from the back and went through him, piercing his heart. He fell forward, but his body was partially suspended above the ground, as the front of the spear was lodged in the ground. Khuroos Khan, who stood a few feet away from him, smiled victoriously. Vikraman ran towards Rangachari. Vedanta Desikar and the sons of Shrutha Prakashikacharya followed Vikraman. Vikraman held Rangachari firmly in his arms, allowing his head to rest on his shoulders. Rangachari's sorrowful eyes looked at Vedanta Desikar. His lips uttered "Om Namo Narayana!", and his soul departed his body.

While Vikraman and Vedanta Desikar stood tearfully, Khuroos Khan commanded two of his soldiers towards Vedanta Desikar. They ran towards Vedanta Desikar with spears in their hands. But before they could reach him, Vikraman felled them with his sword. Khuroos Khan decided to take on Vikraman. A fierce duel ensued. It was Vikraman's rage against Khuroos Khan's ferocity. Vikraman's sword scraped Khuroos Khan's chest. Enraged, Khuroos Khan started to attack Vikraman even more fiercely. Vikraman defended by kneeling on the ground to block Khuroos

Khan's sword. Then he used his strength to push Khuroos Khan aside. Khuroos Khan's sword flew from his hand. Vikraman stood up and proceeded to attack Khuroos Khan with his sword. Khuroos Khan waved towards his men. That's when Vikraman realized he had left Desikar unprotected. He stumbled for a moment, and Khuroos Khan made the most of this opportunity to target Vikraman's hands and disarm him. He then swiftly jumped behind Vikraman and held his neck with one hand. Using his other hand, he held both of Vikraman's hands behind him. Vikraman couldn't break this hold on him. He could see the Khuroos Khan's men running towards Vedanta Desikar. Right then, Khuroos Khan's dagger pierced his neck. Vikraman's vision became blurry and he slowly blacked out. He fell to the ground. Vedanta Desikar stood frozen in shock even as he saw soldiers running towards him.

"Is this the end? Has his time come to go to the abode of the Lord?" - these questions swirled through his mind sending chills down his spine. "What about all the things he had yet to do on this earth?", he thought. His subconscious echoed "This is not the end". On hearing this, the fear on his face vanished, and was replaced with a divine peaceful expression. The enemy soldiers were nearing. The next moment, there was a huge sound that echoed like a giant clap of thunder in the sky. The soldiers running towards Desikar flew in different directions and fell down hard

to the ground. The other soldiers were perplexed by what was happening. The temple elephant Gajendran stood there lifting his trunk up and trumpeting loudly. Soldiers ran towards Gajendran, but were swatted back in all directions. Many of them were trampled to death under Gajendran's mighty feet.

Seeing this, Khuroos Khan ordered his men to bring two elephants from his battalion. He himself mounted one of them. Both elephants now attacked Gajendran. The trumpeting of the elephants echoed in the air like a thousand conch shells being blown in unison. As the elephants attacked each other, it looked like mountains colliding against each other. The men who were caught in between this battle of the elephants were crushed to the ground. Many ran for their lives. The elephants of the Delhi forces wore a shield with iron spikes on their forehead. While the spikes wounded Gajendran, he continued to battle even more fiercely. He beat down one of the elephants to the ground. The elephant on which Khuroos Khan sat attacked Gajendran from behind. As Gajendran turned around, Khuroos Khan jumped on to him and smashed his forehead with a blunt mace he held in his hand. Gajendran fell down to the ground with a loud cry. He looked at the *Ranga Vimana* as he fell. It seemed as though he was saying something to the Lord seated in it. Gajendran's eyes closed as his head hit the ground. As his soul departed, his mountainous body rose up taking one last breath before sinking into stillness. The people of Srirangam shed tears of sorrow seeing him go down. As Gajendran breathed his last, the

Srirangam temple came under the control of the Sultanate. Dead bodies were strewn all around the temple.

Vedanta Desikar, who was looking on at Gajendran's brave fight, realised that it was practically impossible for him to escape. There seemed to be only one thing left to try. He decided to play dead along with the sons of Shrutha Prakashikacharya. He prayed to the Lord, and lay like a dead body among the hundreds of bodies around. After killing Gajendran, Khuroos Khan started to look for Vedanta Desikar. He had noticed that Vedanta Desikar seemed to be the person who had the most protection in the temple. This made him think that Desikar probably knew where Namperumal was located. He inspected each one of the dead bodies. His footsteps approached Desikar. Desikar chanted the name of the Lord in his heart and lay still. Khuroos Khan bent to look closely at Desikar's face, and recognized him. Instinctively, he lifted his sword and aimed at Desikar's head. Desikar's pulse was racing, but he was chanting the Lord's name with every beat of his heart. He laid there motionless.

"Khuroos Khan!!", a commanding voice called from far. It was Ulugh Khan.

"The temple is under our control. Gather your soldiers, we have to search for Namperumal", said Ulugh Khan. Khuroos Khan put his sword back in its sheath and moved on. Desikar breathed a sigh of relief.

At that time, Bhoopathi was standing at the bank of the Kaveri. There was no one else in sight. It looked desolate. There was no boat in sight either. He got into the river and started to swim to the opposite bank. As it was the month of November, the tide was low, and swimming seemed easy. Before he could reach the other bank, he saw some flickering lights like fireflies in the distance. He stopped swimming, but the lights seemed to be coming toward him. As they came close, the 'fireflies' turned into fires lit on wooden sticks. They were being carried by men standing on small boats going towards Srirangam. Some men were swimming alongside the boat as well. Bhoopathi's heart sank as he thought about the prospect of getting caught by the enemies again. But his fears were allayed in the next few seconds. He recognized the men - they were natives of Srirangam who lived and worked in other towns, and were on their way on a visit to their hometown. He swam swiftly towards them.

"Don't go! Stop! Don't go to Srirangam! It is raining fires there! The enemies have killed everyone!", he shouted as loud as he could.

One of the men pointed his torch in Bhoopathi's direction. Kannan was rowing that boat. He stopped rowing immediately. The other boats also stopped.

"Who is that? Oh! It's you, Bhoopathi. What are you saying?", asked Kannan.

Bhoopathi narrated what had happened to everyone. He also claimed that he had fought the enemies, and then escaped. Even so, the people in the boats were furious with him.

"What? You escaped trying to save your life? Giving up Srirangam to our enemies, and living, is not living at all. It is better to die killing as many of them as we can.", said one.

"Yes, it is better to die fighting! Let's go to Srirangam", said the others in unison.

"No, please don't go!" - Bhoopathi's cries were in vain. He reached the bank and sat down looking at the men going towards Srirangam.

"Aren't you ashamed of yourself?" - Bhoopathi was startled and looked around to see who was talking to him. He saw a silhouette standing in the Kaveri. He looked closer. A bolt of lightning revealed the person. It was Rangachari with the spear through him. There was still anger and contempt on his face. He seemed to be asking Bhoopathi a thousand questions.

"Those innocent men believed in a coward like you. How are you going to atone for their deaths? Their enemies did not kill them. It was you who killed them. It was you who killed them!", he said pointedly. Every word pierced Bhoopathi's soul. As tears rolled down his eyes, he ran towards Rangachari. But before Bhoopathi could reach him, Rangachari vanished.

"Giving up Srirangam to our enemies, and living, is not living at all. It is better to die killing as many of them as we can." - hearing this, Bhoopathi turned back. There was a man holding a fire torch in his hand on a boat. It was Rangachari! A few others rose from the water around the boat. They were all followers of Bhoopathi. They looked at Rangachari and said "Yes, it's better to die fighting! Let's go to Srirangam".

Bhoopathi ran towards them. He tried to stop them from going. But all he could grasp at was water from the river. All of them had disappeared into thin air. Bhoopathi sobbed uncontrollably. He felt lost. After about an hour, he proceeded towards Uraiyur.

10. Weaken the Enemy

"Vellaayi!... Vellaayi!"- Namperumal seemed to be calling out to Vellaayi. She awoke. She wasn't sure what time of day or night it was. An oil lamp dimly lit the room. Everyone else in the room was asleep. They had spent about four days in the underground bunker. Vikraman had told them not to get out until they were told to do so. Vellaayi sank into deep thought. She was a bundle of worry, confusion and sorrow, not having any way of knowing what was going on outside.

A gentle breeze blowing on a beautiful evening, anklets clinking at her feet, bangles on her hands, *maruthaani*[40] (*mehndi*) on her palms, wearing a *'thiruman'* (sacred mark) on her forehead and make-up on her eyes, , and dancing before her Lord Namperumal, like a bee around a beautiful flower ... her heart ached as she looked back at those days and wondered if they would ever happen again. Vellaayi was reminded of Rohini's mellifluous singing when Vellaayi would dance. She wondered what Rohini might be doing in the bunker under Srinivasan's house. Perhaps Rohini was also missing the days when they sang and danced together. Vellaayi felt that if she and Rohini had been men, they would have been

---

[40] *An Indian form of body art and temporary skin decoration done using a paste created from the powdered dry leaves of the henna plant.*

fighting - swords in hand - to protect their Lord. She cursed the foolish tradition of sending only men to war. Her train of thought was interrupted by cries of "Vellaayi!... Vellaayi!"...

There was a knocking at the entrance of the bunker. There were three knocks, followed by a pause, followed by another three knocks. Vellaayi felt this could be someone known to her. Noticing that Thiruvengadam had also woken up hearing the sounds, Vellaayi said

"Grandpa! Don't worry. I'll take a look."

She walked towards the corner and started to climb up the wooden stairs that took her closer to the ceiling. She carefully listened for sounds outside.

"I am boatman Kannan", a voice outside the door spoke.

Vellaayi was relieved and removed the latch of the door and pushed it out. Kannan pulled it open from the other side. He wore a gunny bag covering his head. Two more people stood behind him wearing large gunny bags that covered their bodies and faces.

"Kannan! Come in.", said Vellaayi.

Kannan and his two companions came inside. They locked the door behind them and came down into the room. By now, everyone had woken up and stood together. Pillai Lokacharyar stood in front. He was anxious to know what had happened. Everyone held their breath waiting for Kannan to speak. Kannan looked around the room and stopped as his eyes looked into Pillai Lokacharyar's eyes. He broke into tears almost immediately.

"Kannan! Please tell me what happened", asked Pillai Lokacharyar.

"Acharya!", said one of the companions of Kannan as he fell at the feet of Pillai Lokacharyar.

As Pillai Lokacharyar asked "Who is this?", he also recognized who it was.

"Srinivasa", he said as he guided him to stand up and he hugged him tightly. Srinivasan was sobbing uncontrollably. He wiped his tears and narrated the events that had unfolded on the night of the siege by Ulugh Khan. Everyone froze in shock. As he finished the narration of Gajendran dying bravely in the battle, Thiruvengadam asked him, "How did you escape?"

"I was not fortunate enough to become a martyr saving my Lord. To take care of those in the bunker of my house, and also to have someone to pass on the message to you at an appropriate time, Vikraman did not allow me to be in the temple", Srinivasan continued.

"I was in the bunker of my house. I only came out when Kannan came for me. By then, the war was over. The temple is now in the hands of the enemies."

"Where is Desikar?", asked Pillai Lokacharyar anxiously.

Srinivasan's expression relaxed a little. He turned and looked at Kannan. Kannan started to speak.

"When I arrived at Srirangam ferrying some people by boat, it seemed like the war had already ended. But seeing the havoc that was wrought, the people that I had brought there began to attack the enemies in fury - and war broke out once again. I went inside the temple and looked around. When I saw Desikar motionless on the ground, I panicked and screamed. But then I saw his body moving. He actually looked around and motioned me to be quiet. He then told me that he would need to cross the Kollidam river to save the book he had in hand. I took him and his two disciples to Srinivasan's house through the west entrance of the temple."

Then Srinivasan spoke. "They came to my house, and Desikar narrated all that had transpired. Everyone in the bunker seethed in anger, but Desikar consoled them and calmed them down. With about half an hour left to dawn, Kannan and I ferried Desikar and the sons of Shrutha Prakashikacharya to the other bank of Kollidam. They have now travelled towards the forests of Sathyamangalam." This news brought some relief to the people in the room.

Vellaayi listened to everything without batting an eyelid.

"Why did it take so many days for you to get here?", she asked.

Kannan and Srinivasan's faces once again looked downcast. That's when Vellaayi looked at the other person who had accompanied Kannan. Without waiting for an answer, she asked, "Who is this?"

The man lifted the gunny bag from his body. Vellaayi lifted the oil lamp and pointed it towards the man. As light fell upon his face, everyone in the room was shocked.

"Oh! You mean soul! How can you be standing here?", shouted Vellaayi in anger.

It was Bhoopathi, who stood with his head bowed in shame.

"Bhoopathi is not who he used to be. He is a changed man now.", said Kannan.

Before Vellaayi could say anything, Pillai Lokachaarayar interrupted.

"Srinivasa! Please tell us what happened after that", he said.

"When we returned after sending off Desikar, we were in for another shock", said Srinivasan and continued, "There was a fire near the west entrance of the temple. We ran towards the fire, only to see that many of our people were out fighting the enemy instead of hiding in the safety of the bunker. Sadly, they were hacked down easily by the enemy. Some were able to run back into the house. The enemies followed them into the house. As was planned, once the enemies entered the house, the women closed and locked the door of the house, trapping the enemies inside. They had already placed flammable substances near the door, so that no one could escape. They then set the house ablaze using fire-torches. Many of our enemies were thus killed, but many of our people also perished.". Srinivasan was in tears as he finished speaking. He then looked at Vellaayi and said, "The one who set fire to the house, and sacrificed herself in order to kill those enemies, was none other than Rohini."

He wept like he was reliving that moment all over again. Vellaayi couldn't believe her ears. Everything stopped. A thousand volcanoes erupt within her. Her blood boiled. Her face and eyes reddened. Many there felt the same. Tears streamed down Pillai Lokacharyar's cheeks. After a brief silence, Kannan started to speak.

"By the time we got there, everything was over. The enemies had burned down many other houses as well. That's where we found Bhoopathi. He was on the ground injured, crying out in pain.", he said.

Bhoopathi started to speak. "I had reached Uraiyur, but I couldn't be at peace with myself. Rangachari's valour, and the sacrifices being made by the people of Srirangam, haunted me. I was ashamed that I had been such a coward. And so I returned to Srirangam to fight, to try and kill at least a few of our enemies before I die. When I saw people from Srinivasan's house were out fighting, I joined them, and got wounded in the battle. These two saved me.", he said.

Then he added, "I think I'll live the rest of my life repenting all that I've done.".

He then turned towards Vellaayi.

"Vellaayi. Your anger is justified. I've been at my worst behavior with you. It would be wrong on my part to expect you to forgive me. I shall live the rest of my life serving Srirangam. I can only hope that you all forgive me someday.", he said.

"Sincere repentance of one's sins is a mark of a good heart. We all have duties to be done before we leave this earth. Find out what you are meant to do, and fulfil your destiny", said Pillai Lokacharyar. He then looked at Srinivasan and asked, "What is the situation outside now?"

"It is somewhat better. While we were hiding in one of the Devadasi's houses to treat Bhoopathi's wounds, we got some news. Ulugh Khan has apparently gone towards Madurai with a big army of soldiers. However, he has left his most trusted commander Khuroos Khan here along with a small battalion of soldiers - for the sole purpose of finding Namperumal", said Srinivasan.

Those days, Devadasis were quite involved with politics. Many were trained to be spies during times of war, so that they could gather information from soldiers when they visited Devadasi houses for alcohol, dance and entertainment. The Devadasis of Srirangam were doing exactly that.

"We should somehow take Namperumal and leave from here", said Pillai Lokacharyar.

"We thought the enemies would leave after a couple of days, but they're still here. It's almost impossible to leave Srirangam without being spotted by them", said Srinivasan.

"In a few days, we might get an opportunity to escape from here", said Bhoopathi. Everyone looked at him in surprise.

"Spies wear a ring with poison to be used in case they are caught by enemies. They would consume it and die before any information could be extracted from them. Sometimes they would use the poison to kill enemies by mixing it in their food. I had brought the poison from my gold factory in Uraiyur. There are many varieties of poison - some that could kill you instantly and others that would take your life after many hours. When I was in the house of the devadasis, we served poisoned alcohol to a few of the soldiers who were there. The men who consumed it fell unconscious the following day in their tents and died. Since not everyone died, no one suspected the devadasis. They now believe that the deaths were due to some curse. They requested Khuroos Khan's permission to leave Srirangam, but he has not agreed. However, as we keep doing this to more of their people, they are bound to flee Srirangam in a few days. Now we just have to wait for that to happen.", he said.

"What if they come to know about the poison?", asked Thiruvengadam.

No one answered. Srinivasan, Kannan and Bhoopathi looked at each other. They knew they were running out of ideas. After a few moments of silence, Srinivasan spoke.

"It's difficult - in fact, impossible, to take Namperumal across the Kaveri without being spotted by our enemy", said Srirangam.

"Then we shall cross it in front of their very eyes.", said Vellaayi.

"How would that be possible?", asked Thiruvengadam, surprised.

"It is possible. We should be brave enough to take the risk.", Vellaayi started and outlined her plan over the next half an hour. Everyone who heard her out was filled with fear. They were terrified of the consequences if things didn't go as planned.

"No, let's not do this. It's too dangerous. We could end up losing many more lives. More importantly, I don't see how you would escape death yourself.", said Pillai Lokacharyar. Everyone agreed.

"If I die saving Namperumal, I would consider it the greatest gift of my life", said Vellaayi.

"No Vellaayi! This doesn't sound right. You shouldn't put your life at risk.", said Thiruvengadam.

"What else can we do? Should we just wait here till the enemies find us? And hand over Namperumal to them?" - she burst out in rage. Everyone fell silent. Then, breaking the silence in the room, Vellaayi sang a *pasuram*.

Kattu kaṛavai kaṇangaḷ pala kaṛandu

cettaar tiṛal azhiya cennu cerucceyyum

kuttram onnillada kovalartam poṛkoḍiye

puttaravalgul puna mayile! podaray

cuttattu thozhimaar ellaarum vandu nin

muttam puhundu muhil vaṇṇan paer paaḍa

cittade pecaade selva peṇḍaaṭṭi ni

ettukku uṛangam poruḷ elor empaavaay

This was a *pasuram* from the collection of poems that Andal had written in the Thirupaavai. In this hymn, Andal is trying to awaken the *gopika*[41] within her. The *pasuram* is in the form of a question to her, "She who loves the Lord Krishna who goes to the fort of the enemies to destroy them, why do you sleep when people await you at your doorstep?".

---

[41] *A cow herdress of Lord Krishna; also friend or lover of Lord Krishna.*

"The enemy likely expects us to be scared and hiding in fear. They wouldn't expect us to go out bravely before them. We can use this to our advantage", said Vellaayi.

"But there is also the risk of losing more lives…", said Thiruvengdam.

"Grandpa, already thousands of people in Srirangam have given up their lives. My dear friend Rohini killed many enemies before sacrificing herself. I am proud of her. My life is no different to any of theirs. Our duty is to protect Namperumal and Acharya - who will carry Namperumal. If we continue to wait, we will soon be caught. It is better to die fighting rather than die doing nothing at all", said Vellaayi.

There was long contemplation, but no one could come up with a better plan. There was no other way for everyone there but to go with Vellaayi's plan.

As the evening sun was setting the next day, a bullock cart proceeded towards the east entrance of the Srirangam temple. Kannan rode the cart. Inside it, Vellaayi sat dressed in a red saree and wore the ornaments of a Bharatanaatiyam dancer. Pillai Lokacharyar and Thiruvengadam sat beside her. Two men walked behind the cart holding musical instruments. Inside the cart, the casket carrying Namperumal was amongst other boxes containing musical instruments. Srinivasan and Bhoopathi surreptitiously followed them at a safe distance. As it reached the East Uthirai street, the cart turned towards the Kaveri.

Right then, a commanding voice called out "Who is that? Stop there!".

The cart stopped.

11. The East Tower

After the battle, the streets of Srirangam were deserted for a couple of days. After that, a few people - like those who came into Srirangam from different places, the devadasis, and the slaves brought by the Delhi army - tried to go about their daily routine. Still, anyone entering or leaving Srirangam were thoroughly checked by the Sultanate soldiers. If the soldiers felt suspicious of anyone, they would arrest and torture them.

Despite these dangers, Vellaayi, Pillai Lokacharyar and Thiruvengadam were in the bullock cart, acting on Vellaayi's bold plan to sneak Namperumal out of town. Two men walked behind the cart holding musical instruments. Inside the cart, the casket carrying Namperumal lay amongst cases containing musical instruments. Srinivasan and Bhoopathi followed them, unseen by the enemy, a safe distance behind.

"Who is that? Stop there!" - Kannan stopped the cart as soon as he heard that commanding voice. It was the right thing to do - for if he had decided to race ahead, the enemy would have caught up with them before they reached the banks of the Kaveri. It was wiser to stop and answer the questions posed to them. This is what they had decided to do beforehand. Two soldiers approached the cart.

"Who are you? Where are you going?", asked one of them.

"We're going to Uraiyur - to participate in the dance festival at the temple there", said Kannan. The two men who were walking behind the cart came in front. One of the soldiers recognized them as musicians who had performed at a devadasi's house.

"Oh! I recognize you. You can go", said the soldier.

A wave of relief passed through those in the cart, and Kannan got the cart moving. But just as he did, the other soldier said, "Wait! When will you return?".

"Tomorrow"… "After two days".

The two musicians gave two different answers, and this sparked suspicion in the soldier's mind. He walked towards the cart.

"So you don't know when you'll return? What's in the cart?", he asked.

The cart stopped again. Thiruvengadam looked at Vellaayi in horror. Pillai Lokacharyar chanted, eyes closed. Vellaayi sat without any sort of fear or confusion. The soldier looked into the cart. He looked carefully at the people seated inside.

"I haven't seen you before", he said.

"We are from this town. We are coming out for the first time after the war", said Vellaayi. The soldier looked at her closely. Even in that dim light, her face was as radiant as the moon. Her beauty was intoxicating, but the soldier gathered himself quickly.

"Ok, tell me what is in these caskets", he asked.

"Musical instruments and make-up items", said Vellaayi without any hesitation.

"Hmm..can you open them and show me?", asked the soldier.

Vellaayi slowly opened the casket carrying the musical instruments. In one of the caskets there were the beat instruments *nattuvangam* and *thattu manai* used for Bharatanatyam performances. She opened another casket. It had anklets and a few other ornaments that a dancer would wear.

"Hmm.. can you open that one?", he asked, pointing to the casket with Namperumal in it. Thiruvengadam's heart raced and he started to sweat. Vellaayi slowly lifted the casket, placed it on her lap and opened it. The soldier looked inside. He saw.....a white conch shell....surrounded by numerous flowers. Beneath it, wrapped completely in a silk cloth, was Namperumal. However, Namperumal was not visible to anyone looking into the casket. It simply looked like rolled-up silk cloth.

At that moment, footsteps of approaching horses were heard, and everyone's attention turned towards that. Vellaayi swiftly closed the casket and placed it behind the other boxes.

It was Khuroos Khan on a horse, with two of his bodyguards on horses behind him.

"What is going on here?", he asked authoritatively.

The two soldiers standing near the cart bowed to him. Then one of them spoke.

"Chief! These people say they are going to a dance program in Uraiyur. We were inspecting them", he said.

"For a dance program? Who is inside the cart?", asked Khuroos Khan.

"These are people who perform dance programs in the temple", replied the soldier.

"Ask those inside the cart to get down", said Khuroos Khan.

Immediately the soldier ordered the people to get out of the cart. Thiruvengadam, Pillai Lokacharyar and Vellaayi got down from the cart. Khuroos Khan looked at them carefully. His eyes widened on seeing Vellaayi. Her beauty was enchanting. A wave of excitement ran through his body. Without revealing what he was thinking, he started to talk.

"Lady! Where are you going at this hour?", he asked.

She looked straight into his eyes and spoke without hesitation.

"We are going to Uraiyur, for a dance program", she said.

"Would you mind dancing for me?", he asked, laughing.

"I only dance for the Lord. I don't dance for anyone else", she replied pridefully.

"Lady! Watch your words. Don't lose your life unnecessarily", he shouted angrily.

Vellaayi did not respond. She shifted her gaze away from him and looked into the distance.

"There is a temple right here. Let your dance program happen here.", said Khuroos Khan. He then turned towards his soldiers and said, "Take her to the temple, and get her to dance. If she refuses, kill all her companions, and imprison her."

He then rode away on his horse. Pillai Lokacharyar and Thiruvengadam looked at Vellaayi sorrowfully. Their worst fears had come true. However, Vellaayi's face showed no fear whatsoever. She started walking towards the temple. Kannan rode the bullock cart behind her. The others followed suit. They entered the temple through the east entrance. Kannan stood outside the temple with the bullock cart. The others took only the boxes with musical instruments with them into the temple. They left the casket with Namperumal in the cart.

Over the next hour, the *mandap* near the east entrance of Srirangam temple was set up and decorated to stage the dance performance. The musicians tested their instruments and were ready to play. Thiruvengadam sat holding the *nattuvangam* in his hand. Pillai Lokacharyar stood beside a pillar. Their faces betrayed the fear and sorrow that they felt. Vellaayi, fully clad in a dancer's costume, walked towards the center of the *mandap* and stood there. Khuroos Khan's lustful eyes widened trying to take in all her beauty. He wanted to own her, and make her part of his harem. Vellaayi looked at Thiruvengadam. This was his cue to start playing the *nattuvangam*. Vellaayi started with *'alarippu'*, a dance performance that every bharatanatyam dancer starts their performance with. She visualized an image of her mother, who was also her teacher, and the image of Namperumal, who was greater than life itself, and bowed before them. Then Thiruvengadam started to sing hymns from Andal's *Nachiyar Thirumozhi*[42]. He started with the hymn *"Thai oru thingal..."*.

---

[42] *A poem of 143 verses composed by Andal. Thirumozhi literally means "Sacred Sayings" in a Tamil poetic style and "Nachiar" means goddess. Therefore, the title means "Sacred Sayings of the Goddess." This poem fully reveals Andal's intense longing for Vishnu.*

Andal, in the month of January, cleaned her courtyard and decorated it with lovely rangoli. She then prayed to *Kamadevan* (the God of Love) and his brother Saaman and asked them to unite her with Lord Vishnu himself. Vellaayi, performing this dance, expressed Andal's feelings perfectly.

Thai oru tingalum tarai vilakki

tan manddalam ittu maasi munnaal

aiya nun manal konddu teru anindu

azhahinukku alangarittu ananga devaa

uyyavumaangolo enru solli

unnaiyum umbiyaiyum tozhuden

veyyador tazhal umizh sakkarakkai

vengadavarkku ennai vidikkittriye

As Thiruvengadam sang more hymns from the *Nachiyar Thriumozhi*, Vellaayi skilfully brought them to life on stage. The audience was immersed in her performance. Her facial expressions were mesmerizing. The sound from her anklets embellished the hymns, and attracted more people towards the temple. The soldiers guarding the temple also started to pour in, and were lost in her performance.

The emotions conveyed through her expressions and body language while dancing to the lines that described Andal's love for the Lord felt real, because they came from the devotion she had for Namperumal. The lust in Khuroos Khan's eyes grew. His gaze was fixed on her. As all this was going on, two Delhi soldiers approached Pillai Lokacharyar and whispered something to him. He looked at them, surprised. It was Srinivasan and Bhoopathi in disguise. Pillai Lokacharyar left the temple premises with them. No one noticed them leaving. They proceeded towards the bank of the Kaveri carrying the casket with Namperumal in it. A few others came out from the bunker under Thiruvengadam's house and joined them as well. Kannan took them all in his boat and dropped them off at Uraiyur.

Vellaayi was still dancing at the temple. It took her about four full hours to dance to all 143 hymns of *Nachiyar Thirumozhi*. Neither her legs, nor Thiruvengadam's voice, showed any signs of tiredness. However, her anklets seemed to finally tire - they broke and scattered loudly around her on the *mandap*. This seemed to awaken the audience from their trance. Khuroos Khan was shocked as he looked around him. When the dance had started there were only 10 soldiers inside the temple. Now there were hundreds of them there. He was furious. He stood up from his seat and shouted,

"What are you all doing here? How could you let your guard down?", he shouted.

As he spoke, his eyes scanned the temple premises. They stopped at the *mandap*. He was shocked to see that Pillai Lokacharyar was missing.

"Where is the other person who was with you?", he asked, as he walked towards the *mandap*.

Vellaayi and Thiruvengadam were stunned for a moment. Both of them looked at each other. They were praying for Pillai Lokacharyar to have crossed Uraiyur by then. Khuroos Khan came closer to them, his eyes blood-red. A soldier ran towards him -

"Chief! The cart that was standing outside the temple is not there anymore. Two of our soldiers are unconscious on the floor outside the temple.", he said.

Khuroos Khan roared in anger listening to this. He cursed himself for being carried away by the beauty of a woman. He then went up to Vellaayi and grabbed her by her neck. She was breathing heavily after her marathon dance performance. Sweat streamed down her face.

"Lady! Where are the men who were with you? I'm sure you know where Namperumal is. Tell me right now!", he shouted at her.

As he choked her, tears of pain fell from her eyes. She shook her head without wanting to answer his question.

"All you can do is kill me. Go ahead and do it. I won't tell you anything", she stammered.

Khuroos Khan pushed her down onto the floor. His eyes turned to Thiruvengadam. He saw Thiruvengadam's worried face and then turned back to Vellaayi. Vellaayi was looking at Thiruvengadam, and then looked at Khuroos Khan. Khuroos Khan sensed the concern in her eyes. He swiftly pulled out his sword and pressed it against Thriuvengadam's neck. He then looked at Vellaayi.

"Lady, you may not be interested in saving your own life, but if you don't tell me where Namperumal is, each one of your companions will be slaughtered", he said, pointing towards Thiruvengadam and the musicians.

"Child, don't be afraid! Don't tell him anything! Don't worry about me, I'm ready to die!", said Thiruvengadam.

Khuroos Khan raised his sword and swung it towards Thiruvengadam's neck.

"Stop it!... Stop! I'll tell you!...", shouted Vellaayi.

Khuroos Khan stopped. He lowered his sword and slowly walked towards Vellaayi. He used the tip of his sword to lift her head up and asked, "Tell me. Where is Namperumal?"

She lifted her trembling right hand and pointed towards the top floor of the eastern tower. Khuroos Khan looked up towards where she was pointing. "What? On the top floor of the tower? Come with me to the top floor. If Namperumal is not there, everyone here will be dead", he said.

Thiruvengadam was stunned. As Vellaayi led the way, Khuroos Khan followed her.

"No, child, don't go with that demon" said Thiruvengadam, but his words fell on deaf ears.

Vellaayi went up the stairs inside the eastern tower and reached the top floor. A beautiful conch shell was drawn on one of the walls there. She stood there looking at it carefully. Khuroos Khan then reached there behind her.

"Where is Namperumal?", he asked.

Vellaayi turned to look at him. Then she stretched her hand to point towards the streets of Srirangam that were visible from a large opening at the top floor.

"Is this a joke?", asked Khuroos Khan and walked towards the entrance of the opening. The eastern streets of Srirangam were visible clearly from there. He looked around, and then up and down. Nothing seemed unusual. As he turned back furiously towards Vellaayi, a hard blow landed on him, sending him reeling towards the opening. He lost his balance and fell out through the opening. His head hit the ground hard. Khuroos Khan was dead. Vellaayi looked down from the entrance at the top floor. When Khuroos Khan had been distracted, she had prayed to Namperumal, and mustered all her strength to hit him as hard as she could. She was surprised at her own strength. Soldiers ran outside the temple hearing the sound. They were shocked to see Khuroos Khan lying dead in a pool of blood. They started to climb up the stairs towards the top floor.

"Vellaayi!", someone called out. It was the voice of Namperumal! Vellaayi turned and ran towards the voice. She looked down towards the inside of the temple. The scene gave her goosebumps. It wasn't night anymore - the morning sun shone brightly. A mother stood there with a baby in her arms. Vellaayi looked carefully. It was her mother Ponni. She realized that the baby was none other than Vellaayi herself. The baby looked up at Vellaayi at the top of the tower, and laughed with excitement. Now Vellaayi looked up at the sky. The scene changed again. The *Ranga Vimana* shone brightly under a moonlit sky. She brought her hands together to pray to the *Ranga Vimana*. She could hear the footsteps of the soldiers approaching the top floor. They were very near. She closed her eyes. She saw yet another scene in her mind. She was standing atop a hill and looking down upon a ferocious ocean. She could hear Namperumal.

"Come, Vellaayi. Why are you afraid of the *Thirupaarkadal*? The time has come for you to join me. Come on.", he said.

As she looked at the ocean again, it appeared to be peaceful and serene. As if in a trance, she kept walking. Her feet crossed the edge of the tower opening. She was falling, but she felt like she was floating in water. Through the darkness, she could see a light approaching her. Her eyes couldn't look directly at it as it came closer. She closed her eyes. Namperumal appeared from within the light. He was dressed in a groom's attire. He threw a garland around her neck and pulled her towards him. Then as he sprinkled some water onto her face, she opened her eyes. Namperumal stood before her smiling gently. She fell at his feet and sought his blessings. He lifted her and offered a garland around her neck. Vellaayi smiled gently at Namperumal.

That very moment, people were shocked to see Vellaayi fall to the ground. She laid there dead - but her lips wore a gentle smile.

The soldiers who had reached the top floor could not piece together what had happened there. All they could see was the conch shell drawn on the wall of the top floor. They couldn't explain how Khuroos Khan and Vellaayi both fell to their deaths from two different sides of the tower. They concluded that the deaths were caused by the same 'unknown force' that had mysteriously killed many soldiers in their army. Fear spread among their ranks, and they left Srirangam. They set up their new base near Kannanur, beyond the northern bank of Kollidam river.

Meanwhile, Bhoopathi and Kannan returned to Srirangam after dropping off the group carrying

Namperumal at Uraiyur. That group, led by Pillai Lokacharyar, proceeded towards Madurai. They stopped at a place called Jyothiskudi and rested for a while. Pillai Lokacharyar's heart was heavy as he thought about those who sacrificed their lives in Srirangam. He prayed to the Lord for liberation from his sorrow. That night, his soul departed and reached the holy abode of Lord Vishnu. Srinivasan then took charge of the group and led them ahead. By this time, the Pandian kings were defeated by the Sultanate forces, who took over the kingdom. Hence, the group with Namperumal decided against going to Madurai. They left for Malabar instead. After a few days, they reached the temple at Tirupathi and placed Namperumal there. No one in Srirangam knew where Namperumal was.

Jalaluddin Ahsan Khan became the ruler of Madurai under the Sultanate forces. Ulugh Khan returned to Delhi. He became the emperor of Delhi after his father. He was renamed Mohammad Bin Tuglaq once he became king. His ascension created a lot of friction and power struggles within the kingdom. Hence his attention was diverted from Srirangam. Normalcy started to return to Srirangam. The people of Srirangam made a procession deity similar to Namperumal and earnestly resumed the temple rituals. However, they did not have the means to conduct the rituals with the same pomp and grandeur of the past. Over time, the temple deteriorated without proper maintenance.

About twelve years later, a new kingdom was formed on the banks of river Tungabadra. Harihara and Bukka created an empire and fought against the Sultanate forces. When the people of Srirangam heard about this, they went to meet King Bukka along with holy water from river Kaveri and river Thamirabarani in Madurai. They requested the King to help them restore the temple to its old glory. He promised to help them once the war with the Delhi forces was over. His queen was pregnant with their first child at that time. She drank the holy water the people had brought with them. The baby in her womb as well drank the holy water. They were blessed with a baby boy who, in time, would come to be known as the brave Kumara Kampanna. From the time he was a child, he had a soft corner for the kingdom of Madurai. As a teenager, he fought many wars commanding his father's troops. When King Bukka contemplated sending a force to free Madurai, Kumara Kampanna came forward and asked for permission to lead the force. King Bukka gave his nod. Kumara Kampanna led the force to Madurai.

The story of his battle against the Sultanate forces that controlled Madurai has been chronicled by his wife Gangadevi in her book Madhura Vijayam.

First, Kumara Kampanna defeated Arcot Nawab and captured the fort. His prime minister Gopanna was instrumental in winning the battle. That night, as Kumara Kampanna slept in the Arcot fort, he had a dream. In his dream, he was standing in the middle of a beautiful garden. He saw someone waving at him from afar. He went towards the person. It was a seven-year-old girl, whom we know as Vellaayi. She stood there sorrowfully, her eyes filled with tears. His heart melted.

"Child, why did you call me? What can I do for you?", he asked.

Vellaayi did not answer. She just ran through the bushes in the garden and disappeared from his sight. Kumara Kampanna followed her. As he made his way through the bushes, the entire scene changed. The girl was standing in the middle of a dilapidated *mandap*. Behind her was a statue of Lord Vishnu in the *Ananthasayanam* pose. The roof of the *mandap* was broken. This visual shocked Kumara Kampanna. Vellaayi started to speak.

"O King! Lord Arangan's temple does not have a roof. The rituals in Madurai Meenakshi Amman temple have been stalled for many months. You should recover Srirangam and Madurai to its past glory", she said, overcome with emotion. She then disappeared into thin air.

Kumara Kampanna believed that the goddess Meenakshi from Madurai temple had appeared as a small girl and told him what needed to be done. The next day, he sent Gopanna with a small force towards Srirangam. He led the remaining forces towards Madurai and defeated the Sultan. He made the Pandya dynasty rule Madurai once again. All the rituals at the Madurai Meenakshi temple were resumed in a grand manner - just like the old days.

Gopanna defeated the enemies stationed at Kannanur. He captured the fort there. He then reached Srirangam. He saw that people of Srirangam were worried about the whereabouts of Namperumal. Gopanna was an ardent devotee of Lord Vishnu in Tirupathi. He recollected seeing Namperumal in Tirupathi earlier. He immediately ordered for Namperumal to be brought back to Srirangam. The restoration work of Srirangam temple began. All the damaged parts of the temple were repaired and rebuilt. Kumara Kampanna visited Srirangam temple for the grand festival. Bhoopathi and Kannan who had become very old now, narrated the story of the war of Srirangam and the sacrifice made by Vellaayi many years ago. Kumara Kampanna was overwhelmed and moved to tears when he heard the story. He looked at the grand east tower before him. The eastern tower's renovation work was almost complete. The tower was painted white, and the painting of colors over it was pending. For a moment he thought he saw a woman standing on the top floor of the east tower. He felt goosebumps all over his body, and a thought occurred to him.

"Gopanna, Vellaayi's sacrifice was as great as this tower. The white colour on it could be a tribute to her name Vellai Ammal - which stands for 'one who is as pure as white'. In her honour, we could leave this tower painted white", said Kampanna.

"That's a very noble thought, my prince! We shall do as you say.", said Gopanna.

Hearing this, Bhoopathi and Kannan were overwhelmed. Happy tears rolled down their wrinkled cheeks.

Thus, Namperumal finally returned to Srirangam after a gap of 48 years. The people of Srirangam decorated Namperumal and performed the temple rituals in a grand manner. There were special rituals as well. Everyone participated in the festivities and celebrated their dear Lord. During this auspicious time, Vedanta Desikar returned to Srirangam. He was filled with happiness at being able to pray to Lord Arangan and Namperumal once again. He wrote a poem in praise of Gopanna and had it inscribed on the wall of the temple.

At the same time Vellaayi was standing on the top floor of the east tower. She was thrilled seeing Namperumal and the festivities in Srirangam. She folded her hands and prayed to Namperumal - the love of her life.

A Telugu poet named Namburi Kesavachaaryar has written about Vellaayi's sacrifice in his work Acharya Sukthi Mukthavali. Even today, many believe in the legend of the east gopuram being painted white in honor of Vellaayi's sacrifice. Those who visit Srirangam today can actually see the replica of Namperumal that was made when Namperumal was not in Srirangam. The replica is now placed near the Namperumal and Ranganayaki statues.

Namperumal lives on in the hearts of the people of Srirangam, and enjoys a special place in their homes, blessing them with all prosperity.

||Om Namo Narayanaya||

Epilogue

We would like to express our sincere thanks to you for reading this novel about Vellaayi's bravery and her devotion to the Lord. Although the novel is based on true incidents, we have taken the creative liberty to fill in the missing pages from history with fiction. It is not our intention to hurt anyone's sentiments by doing this. While this story does highlight Vellaayi's supreme sacrifice, it is just one example of the enormous devotion and love the people of Srirangam have for their Lord Arangan. If you turn the pages of the history of Srirangam, you will find many others like Vellaayi. The streets of Srirangam, the walls of the temple, the inscriptions on the rocks, all tell us many such stories even today. Srirangam has something unique compared to all other holy places with temples of Lord Vishnu - the fact that the people of Srirangam don't consider Lord Arangan as God, they consider Him as part of their own family.

Many history books helped us in the creation of this novel. We have listed them here for the benefit of those interested in learning more about the history involved.

- Sources of Vijayanagar History, S. Krishnaswamy Iyengar

- Madhura Vijayam, Sree Ganga Devi

- Naachiyaar Thirumozhi, Sree Andal

- Nithyasumangali: Devadasi Tradition in South India, Sasika C. Kersenboom

- A History of South India: From prehistoric times to the fall of Vijayanagar, K.A. Neelakanta Sastry

- Kovil Ozhugu, Srirangam Temple

We wholeheartedly thank the authors of all these books.

|| Om Namo Narayanaya ||

With lots of Love

K.V. Raja Saravanan

and

Naveen Ithikkat

Glossary

Aadi

The fourth month of the Tamil Calendar, which marks the onset of monsoons

Aarti

A Hindu religious ritual of worship, in which light is offered to one or more deities

Abaranji

'Purest' gold

Acharyar

Expert instructor in matters such as religion, or any other subject

Adhirasam

A type of Indian sweet

Ananthasayanam

Literally meaning "sleeping on the serpent named Ananta", it is a symbolic representation of the cosmic balance of finity within infinity.

Andal

The only female Alvar among the 12 Alvar saints of South India. The Alvar saints are known for their affiliation to the Vaishnava tradition of Hinduism

Angavasthiram

Traditional rectangular white piece of cloth or stole, worn by men from the Hindu community, which is draped over the shoulders.

Brahma Sutra

Another name for Vedanta Sutras

Champak

Magnolia champaca, an evergreen tree known for its fragrant flowers

Dharma

Religious and moral law governing individual conduct (as per Hinduism)

Ekadesi

A Sanskrit word for number 11, indicating the 11th day of each half of the month in the Vedic lunar calendar. It is considered a day to cleanse the body, aid repair and rejuvenation and is usually observed by partial or complete fast.

Getti Melam

Traditional wedding tune played on the 'nadaswaram' drums

Gopika

A cow herdress of Lord Krishna; also friend or lover of Lord Krishna.

Gopuram

monumental entrance tower, usually ornate, at the entrance of a Hindu temple in Southern India

Kumkum

A red powder, made from saffron or turmeric, used ceremonially by Hindu women to make various markings on the body

Mandap

A covered structure with pillars

Mangal sutra

A necklace that the groom ties around the bride's neck in the Indian subcontinent

Mangala Aarti

Daily predawn worship ceremony honoring the Deity of the Supreme Lord, which brings auspiciousness (mangala) to the performer.

Margazhi

The ninth month of the Tamil Calendar, which has more festivals and events than other months

Maruthaani/Mehndi

An Indian form of body art and temporary skin decoration done using a paste created from the powdered dry leaves of the henna plant.

Maund

An Indian unit of weight equal to about 82 pounds (37 kg)

Mudra

A symbolic hand gesture typically used in Indian dance.

Mutt

Sanskrit word that means institute or college or monastery

Nachiyar Thriumozhi

A poem of 143 verses composed by Andal. Thirumozhi literally means "Sacred Sayings" in a Tamil poetic style and "Nachiar" means goddess. Therefore, the title means "Sacred Sayings of the Goddess." This poem fully reveals Andal's intense longing for Vishnu.

Namaskaram

Namaste / namaskar / namaskaram is a customary, non-contact form of Hindu greeting.

Nithya sumangali

Female who is married to the Lord and thus would never be a widow.

Pann

Melodic mode used by the Tamil people in their music since ancient times.

Pooja

Act of worship

Punnai

Tamil name for Alexandria Laurel trees - evergreen ornamental trees cultivated in tropical areas

Ranga Vimana

The shrine over the sanctum sanctorum of the temple at Srirangam

Rangoli

Indian art form, in which patterns are created on the floor or the ground using materials such as coloured rice, coloured sand, quartz powder or flower petals

Sudarshana Chakra

A spinning, disk-like weapon literally meaning "disk of auspicious vision," having 108 serrated edges used by Lord Vishnu.

Sultanate

Region governed by a Sultan (Muslim king)

Tapta Mudra

A heated metal symbol (made of copper or gold) depicting a conch and the Sudarshana Chakra, that is stamped/applied on the body.

Thirupaavai

Tamil devotional poem by Andal. It is a part of Divya Prabandha, a collection of the works of the twelve Alvars, that is considered an important part of the devotional genre of Tamil literature.

Thiruparkadal

Heavenly ocean surrounding Vishnu's abode in heaven

Thulabharam

An ancient Hindu practice in which a person is weighed against a commodity (such as gold, grain, fruits or other objects), and the equivalent weight of that commodity is offered as donation.

Treta Yuga

The second of the four yugas, or ages of mankind, in Hinduism.

Vaikunta Ekadesi

A special Ekadasi dedicated to Vishnu. It occurs in the Hindu calendar, in the month of Margashirsha (between December and January). When observed, it bestows liberation from the cycle of birth and death.

Vedanta Sutra

The Vedanta Sutras (also called the Brahma Sutras) were written by the sage Vyasa (Badarayana) to systematise the teachings of the Upanishads. Upanishads are philosophical texts delineating some of the key concepts within Hinduism, including notions of the soul, reincarnation, karma, and liberation.

Vedas

The most ancient Hindu scriptures, written in early Sanskrit. The four chief collections of Vedas are the Rig Veda, Sama Veda, Yajur Veda, and Atharva Veda.